A MARRIAGE MADE IN HEAVEN

Without thinking, simply because her terror about what had occurred was still with her, Samala ran towards the Duke and flung herself against him.

"You . . . are safe!"

Her hands had reached up towards the Duke's neck, and as he put his arms around her she held onto him frantically.

He looked down at her, her eyes misty with tears, her lips trembling, and he thought no one could be lovelier.

Then his lips came down on hers.

For a moment Samala could not believe it was happening.

Then she felt she must have died and he had carried her into a Heaven where there were only flowers and music and love. . . .

A Marriage
Made in Heaven

Barbara Cartland

A Marriage Made in Heaven

First Published in United States 1982
ⓒ 1982 Barbara Cartland
This Edition Published by **Book Essentials South** 1999
Distributed by **BMI**, Ivyland, PA 18974
PRINTED IN THE UNITED STATES OF AMERICA
ISBN 1-57723-415-4

Author's Note

In the United Kingdom, the heir to an hereditary peerage or baronetcy usually inherits not only the Dukedom, Marquisate, Earldom, Viscountcy, or Barony, but also the ancestral home and the family fortune.

The right of primogeniture, whereby the eldest son inherits practically everything, was designed to preserve the Estates intact and undivided and thus ensure a fitting background for each successive heir.

In the same way, the paintings, furniture, silver, and other articles of value in the family home were all entailed onto the next heir, so that he could not sell them and dissipate the family fortune.

Titles normally descend in the male line only, so that if the head of the family has no son, his male next of kin, who may be only a cousin, is his heir presumptive.

It is a fact that in the case of a few ancient peerages, both English and Scottish, the succession can, in default of a male heir, fall to a female. But this occurs only when this right of succession has been granted specifically at the time of the creation of each peerage.

Chapter One

1827

The Duke of Buckhurst brought his team of horses to a standstill outside the impressive f t door of his house in Park Lane.

As he did so, he pulled his watch from his waistcoat pocket and said in a tone of satisfaction:

"One hour, fifty-two minutes! A record, I think, Jim!"

"Two minutes better than last time, Your Grace," Jim said from his seat at the back of the Phaeton.

With a smile on his rather hard lips, the Duke stepped out onto the red carpet which had been hastily run down the steps by two white-wigged footmen wearing the distinctive family livery.

The Duke walked into the marble Hall with its magnificent double staircase rising to the First Floor, and a Butler took his tall hat and driving-gloves.

"The Marchioness and Lady Bredon are in the Salon, Your Grace," he said respectfully.

"Damn!" the Duke ejaculated under his breath.

He was about to turn in a different direction when

there were footsteps behind him, and his brother-in-law, the Marquis of Hull, came in through the open door.

"Hello, Buck, I see you have arrived!" the Marquis exclaimed unnecessarily.

"What is going on," the Duke enquired, "a family conclave?"

"I am afraid so," the Marquis answered.

The Duke of Buckhurst's lips tightened, but he did not say anything for the moment. Then he remarked:

"Tell my sisters I am back, Arthur, and will not keep them waiting long, and see that the champagne gets them into a better mood than I anticipate they would be otherwise."

The Marquis of Hull did not laugh, he merely walked rather pompously towards the Salon, while the Duke went up the staircase and into his own rooms.

He had been told that his sisters wished to see him while he was in the country, and he was already expecting that as usual they would be reproaching him for some misdemeanour.

While he considered it none of their business, he was well aware from experience that they would be very voluble on the subject.

The Duke's two sisters were older than he was, and when he arrived in the world as the answer to his father's dreams and ambitions, he had been in most people's opinion abominably spoilt from the time he was in the cradle.

Certainly his two sisters had done their best to spoil him, and the task was completed, as soon as he grew up, by innumerable beautiful women who pursued him, pandered to his every whim, and were prepared to entrust him not only with their hearts but with their reputations.

It was not surprising, since he was exceedingly handsome, rich, and the head of one of the most important families in the country, that the Duke was not

2

only spoilt but had a reputation as a roué that had made his name a byword in Society.

Because it was impossible for anything to be hidden from gossip-mongers, he was a Cartoonist's delight, and a newspaper was seldom published without making some reference to him in their columns, so that the populace looked on him as a figure they could admire, envy, and applaud.

When he appeared on the race-course he was cheered from one end of it to the other much more loudly than the King, which was not surprising, and whenever he drove down Piccadilly he was admired not only by the *Beau Monde* but by every crossing-sweeper.

" 'E's not only a sportsman but a man!" one lorry-driver was heard to say, and that just about summed up the Duke's attraction.

It was inevitable that he should, in the opinion of those who considered themselves to be pillars of Society, go too far.

His love-affairs, which multiplied and remultiplied every year, needed little exaggeration to make them scandalous, and the mothers of débutantes, though ambitious for a distinguished and aristocratic son-in-law, hurried their girls away from the man they feared might contaminate them.

These precautions were quite unnecessary since the Duke was not interested in young girls, preferring sophisticated women whose husbands were either too complacent or too cowardly to object to the time he spent with their wives.

Nevertheless, the members of his family incessantly worried about the gossip that the Duke evoked with everything he did, and were even more worried that at thirty-four he showed no signs of settling down and providing an heir to the title and the Estates.

As the Duke changed from his driving-clothes he thought with a cynical twist of his lips that when he went downstairs he would undoubtedly hear the usual long-drawn-out plea for him to marry and live a more conventional life.

"Why the devil should I?" he asked aloud, and his valet, who was helping him dress and had been with him for many years, did not respond, knowing that the Duke was talking to himself and not to him.

"Tomorrow I am going to Newmarket, Yates," the Duke said, "and as I shall want you there when I arrive, you had better leave in the brake an hour before I do."

"I anticipated that, Your Grace," Yates replied, "and I've got everything packed."

"Good!"

However, the Duke was thinking of something quite different as he left his bedroom to walk slowly down the stairs.

No man could have looked smarter or more magnificent.

Although the Duke would have been extremely annoyed if he had been told that he was a "Dandy," he was undoubtedly a *"Beau,"* or perhaps his nickname of "Buck," which had been his ever since he was a School-boy, suited him better.

The difference between him and those who slavishly strived to be a "Tulip of Fashion" was that he wore his clothes, which fitted him to perfection, as if they were part of himself and he was completely unconscious of them.

At the same time, no-one wore more skilfully or more elegantly tied cravats, and Yates knew the polish on his master's Hessian boots was the envy of every other valet in the *Beau Monde*.

The Duke reached the Hall, and as the front door was open and he saw the spring sunshine outside and a slight wind moving the young, green leaves of the trees in Hyde Park, he had a sudden impulse to go back to the country and not face his family who were waiting for him.

If there was one thing he disliked more than

anything else, it was the reproaches and recriminations of his sisters.

While they were too afraid of him to say as much as they really wanted to, the Duke was quite certain that the next half-an-hour would be an uncomfortable one in which, whether he liked it or not, he would be on the defensive.

'Damn them! Why can they not leave me alone?' he thought as the Butler hurried ahead to open the door of the Salon.

He walked into the room, conscious that there was a sudden silence as he did so, which obviously meant that the three members of his family had just been talking about him.

His elder sister, the Marchioness of Hull, had been a great beauty as a girl, and her marriage to the Marquis had been considered most appropriate and an excellent match.

His second sister, Margaret, had married Lord Bredon, who was considerably older than she was, and he was not only exceedingly wealthy but an important Member of the House of Lords and had a very enviable position at Court.

Now as three pairs of eyes watched him, the Duke walked across the Aubusson carpet, thinking as he went that while at times they irritated and annoyed him, his family was a very attractive one and he had every reason to be proud of them.

"How are you, Elizabeth?" he asked, kissing the Marchioness on the cheek.

Before she could reply, he kissed his younger sister and walked away from them to where there was champagne waiting for him on a silver tray.

He poured himself out a glass of it, then returned the bottle to the ice-cooler and said with a smile:

"All right, I am listening! What have I done now to bring you here with faces like those of Methodist

Preachers and undoubtedly words of condemnation on your lips?"

The Marchioness, who had a greater sense of humour than her sister, laughed.

"Oh, Buck, that is just the sort of thing you would say! But this time we have not come to talk about you, but about Edmund."

"Edmund?" the Duke asked in a dry voice. "What has he done now?"

"You will hardly believe it when we tell you," Lady Bredon replied.

The Duke settled himself comfortably in the high-backed chair opposite the sofa on which his two sisters were seated.

"If Edmund is in money trouble again," he said, "I do not intend to pay his debts."

"It is worse than that," the Marchioness said.

"Worse than debt?" the Duke asked in surprise.

His cousin Edmund was the heir presumptive to the Dukedom and was cordially disliked by the whole family.

He was in fact a very unpleasant creature who not only battened on the Duke for money, but also exceeded every accepted rule of decent behaviour in taking every possible advantage of his family connections.

He was shrewd and crafty and dishonest in small ways, and being also consumed with envy, hatred, and malice, he decried the Duke on every possible occasion, although he was quite prepared to live on any money he could extract from him.

There was silence, and now the Duke enquired:

"Well? What has Edmund been up to? It cannot be much worse than what he has done already."

"He has got married!" the Marquis of Hull said bluntly.

The Duke started and stared at his brother-in-law as if he could not believe what he had heard.

"Married?" he exclaimed. "Who would marry Edmund?"

"Lottie Linkley," the Marquis said briefly.

The Duke looked as if the name meant nothing to him. Then he gave an exclamation and his expression altered.

"Lottie Linkley!" he repeated. "You do not mean . . . ?"

"I do," the Marquis confirmed, "and Edmund has not only married her, but has also announced to all and sundry that she is already having a baby!"

"I can hardly believe that what you are telling me is the truth," the Duke said. "Lottie with child!"

He spoke beneath his breath, and the Marquis said:

"I had not heard of her for so long that I thought she must be much older than she is. But her actual age, according to Edmund, is thirty-one."

The Duke drank his champagne as if he needed it.

As he did so he was thinking that the last time he had seen Lottie Linkley was when she was performing at a Regimental Dinner which one of his friends had given in a Private Room at one of the "Houses of Pleasure."

It had been a very wild evening, at which the drink was excellent and plentiful, and every gentleman present had an extremely attractive young woman at his side.

But the *pièce de résistance* came with the port, when an enormous cake, covered with candles representing the number of years since the Regiment had been formed, was carried in and placed in the centre of the table.

As the Senior Officer present, it had been the Duke's privilege to blow out the candles, and then a sword was handed to him in order to cut the cake.

As he was about to do so, the top of it was thrown back and Lottie, wearing little more than a few feathers in the Regimental colours, came up like Venus rising from the foam, and proceeded to sing an amusing but

7

exceedingly vulgar song to which most of those present knew the chorus.

There was no doubt that she looked very attractive, in a theatrical manner, and voluptuously seductive.

But there was no need for the Duke's sisters to tell him that the idea of her eventually becoming the Duchess of Buckhurst was unthinkable.

"Edmund has been saying," the Marquis continued, "that as there is no chance of your providing an heir to the title after you announced yourself to be an avowed bachelor, he is determined to make certain of the succession, and they are already making bets at White's as to whether Lottie's child will be a boy or a girl."

The Duke rose to his feet.

"Dammit!" he exclaimed. "This is too much!"

"That is what we hoped you would think, dearest Buck," his sister Elizabeth said. "And you do realise there is only one thing you can do?"

"Get married!" Margaret added unnecessarily.

The Duke was already aware that that was what they were insinuating, and now he walked away from them towards the window to look out into the garden at the back of the house.

It had been skilfully laid out to make the best possible display of flowers, shrubs, and trees in the limited space available, but what he saw was not the gold of the daffodils or the first white and purple lilac blossom, but the great trees in the Park at Buckhurst.

Behind them stood the house, which, redesigned and redecorated by his grandfather fifty years earlier, had existed on the same foundations for four centuries.

There had been members of the family who had served their country as Statesmen and many more who had been great Generals and distinguished Admirals.

But while many of them had been rakes and roués like himself, none had ever in the history of the family made somebody like Lottie Linkley his wife, and the

8

thought of her taking his mother's place was to the Duke abhorrent.

In the silence behind him he knew that his sisters' eyes were watching him, and they were almost holding their breath, waiting for his reply. He could not help thinking resentfully that Edmund had dealt them a trump card.

He had lost count of how many times Elizabeth and Margaret had begged him almost on bended knee to get married and start a family.

He had always been able to laugh at them and tell them that there was plenty of time, and anyway he preferred being a bachelor and would doubtless remain one until he died.

It amused him to defy them and say publicly that marriage was not for him and that no woman would ever get him to the altar. In fact, it had become a regular joke to refer to him as "Buck the Bachelor"!

There had even been talk of starting a "Bachelors' Club," with him as the Chairman.

Now he realised too late that while most of his friends had known he was only joking or rather putting off the evil hour when he must take a wife, Edmund had taken him seriously.

'It is just the sort of thing he would do!' the Duke thought irritably to himself.

Then he thought that only Edmund would marry somebody like Lottie and imagine that if he did inherit the title, people would accept her as the Duchess of Buckhurst.

Yet, he knew that once Edmund was the Duke, he would not worry about the social scandal he caused, secure in the knowledge that the Estates and possessions which were entailed onto the heir to the Dukedom must become his.

Edmund had always been obsessed by money, and although he had quite enough on which to live comfortably as an ordinary young Man-About-Town, he had been almost insanely extravagant, confident that rather than accept the scandal of his being dunned and taken to prison, his cousin would pay up for him.

The Duke had paid, and paid again, and the last time, which was a little over a month ago, he had said to Edmund categorically:

"You must understand that this is the last time! I have no intention of providing you with one more penny to throw down the inexhaustible drain of your expenditure on wine, gaming, and women!"

"It is what you enjoy yourself," Edmund had replied impertinently.

"Whatever I do or do not do," the Duke said sharply, "I can afford to pay my own way. But remember that as head of the family I have to dispense the family fortune fairly amongst those who require assistance."

He saw the scornful twist on Edmund's lips and added:

"Good God, man! Do you not realise what the Estate spends on Alms Houses, Orphanages, and Pensions? The sum is astronomical! At the same time, it is our duty to provide for those who have served us in the past, and I do not intend to allow you to deplete the Exchequer for your own selfish ends."

"Really, Cousin!" Edmund replied. "I cannot believe that you, of all people, are preaching to me! Do you realise what your reputation is, and what people say about you behind your back?"

"I am not in the least concerned with that," the Duke said loftily, "and my extravagances are not entirely concerned, as yours are, with losing money in cheap Gaming-Houses, and spending it on women whose profession it is to leave your pockets empty."

"High-flown words!" Edmund jeered. "We did not all start life with your advantages."

The Duke realised that there was no use talking to his cousin any further.

He merely repeated that this was the last time he

would bail him out, and the next time he got into debt he would have to sell up or go to the Debtors' Prison, and he would do nothing to help him.

Edmund had not even expressed any thanks for the very large sum of money he received to settle his outstanding debts. Instead, he had struck back in a way that the Duke thought none of them could have anticipated, and it was undoubtedly very effective.

He had suspected for some time that Edmund was trying to borrow money on the security that he was the heir presumptive to the Dukedom, although seeing that the Duke himself was still a young man, the Money-Lenders would not be over-anxious to lend on what was no more than an outside chance.

But there were always those who would gamble on the fact that he had declared he preferred to remain a bachelor and was never seen in public or at private parties with a girl who might be considered a suitable wife for a Duke.

Now the dreaded moment had come, and he knew, without his sisters putting it into words, that he would have to do something about it.

Just for a moment he thought he would be damned if he would conform just to please them or to defeat Edmund.

Then he thought of Lottie Linkley sitting in his mother's place at the end of the table, wearing the Buckhurst jewels and sleeping in the bed which had been occupied by the Duchesses of Buckhurst for centuries, and he knew it was something he could not allow.

And, quite apart from anything else, the Duchess of Buckhurst was by tradition a Lady of the Bedchamber to the Queen.

The silence in the room behind him had become oppressive, and the Duke turned round.

"Very well," he said, and his voice was harsh, "you win! I will get married!"

Elizabeth Hull gave a cry of delight, sprang to her feet, and, running to her brother, threw her arms round him and kissed his cheek.

"I knew, dearest, you would see sense!" she said. "Although I am aware you have always hated the idea, I am sure you will find somebody beautiful to be your Duchess and you will be very happy with her."

The Duke took her arms from his neck and walked once again to the table to pour himself another glass of champagne.

"*I* will not find her," he said. "As this is your idea, I have no intention of having any part in it."

"What do you mean?" Margaret asked. "I do not understand."

The Duke filled his glass before he answered:

"Let us be practical, if nothing else. I cannot remember when I last met a young girl whom I imagine you would consider suitable as the future Duchess of Buckhurst, and I have neither the time nor the inclination to go looking for one."

"Then how are you to be married?" Margaret enquired.

"That is your business, and yours alone," the Duke answered. "You have all been nagging me to find a wife for the last five—or it is ten?—years. Very well, find one!"

"B-but how can we . . . ?" Margaret began, only to be interrupted by her sister.

"Are you really saying," Elizabeth asked, "that you expect us to choose the woman you will marry?"

"Either that, or Edmund can instal Lottie Linkley at Buckhurst Park and here, and doubtless enjoy racing my horses at Newmarket."

Elizabeth gave a cry of horror as she said:

"No, no! Of course that must not happen! Of course, dearest, we will help you in your quest in every way we can."

"It is not a question simply of help," the Duke said

in a hard voice. "You have told me it is my duty to marry, and I suppose in the circumstances there is nothing else I can do. But I will have no part in it! You will find my future Duchess and I will marry her to ensure the succession, but apart from that I intend to live my own life as I always have."

His sister gave a little cry of horror.

"Oh, Buck, you cannot mean that!"

"I do mean it!" the Duke said. "You know as well as I do that the very idea of marriage has always appalled me as an intolerable restriction and an inmitigated bore."

"It need not be . . ." Elizabeth replied.

The Duke laughed, but there was no humour in the sound.

"My dear Elizabeth, look round you. How many of our friends do you think are really happy, and how many wives with any pretentions to looks are faithful to their husbands?"

As he spoke he thought of all the married women who had fallen all too eagerly into his arms, apparently without one thought for the man to whom they were married or for the breaking of their marriage vows.

One reason why the Duke was so firmly opposed to marriage was that he despised the men who were cuckolded by their wives, and he felt that the humiliation of it was something to which he would never subject himself.

Every time he left another man's house, having made love to his wife, he was aware that he had insulted and degraded a member of his own sex.

Although he knew that most of his contemporaries would laugh at him for having such ideas, he had always been determined that he would never be in such a position himself.

If he married and found that his wife was unfaithful to him, he thought he would throttle her and kill the man who had seduced her.

"There is only one thing on which I insist," he said now, "and that is that the girl I marry is very young and, as far as can be ascertained, pure and untouched by any other man."

"But of course! That goes without saying!" his sister Margaret remarked.

The Duke's lips curved in a cynical smile.

He was thinking of the number of women to whom he had made love who had told him how they had first been seduced either by their Riding-Masters or their Music-Teachers.

Others had admitted quite frankly to a number of lovers with whom they had deceived their husbands long before he had come into their lives.

Such confessions had given him a low opinion of women, even while they fascinated and at times infatuated him, but he put them only one step above the "Cyprians" and "Bits of Muslin" who sold their favours.

In fact, he often told himself that the latter were more honest than those who practised deception with an agility that seemed to have been born in them.

"Are you really saying," Elizabeth said, as if she wanted to have it clear in her mind, "that Margaret and I, with of course Arthur's help, must find you a suitable wife who is not only well enough bred to marry into the family but is also a young and innocent girl?"

"The answer to that, putting it concisely, is 'yes'!" the Duke replied. "I do not want to be worried with her, I have no intention of courting her, and I suggest that as it is now the second of May, you arrange the wedding to take place on the second of June. That will leave me plenty of time to take my horses to Ascot and win, as I intend to do, the Gold Cup this year."

There was a silence of sheer astonishment. Then the Marquis said:

"Surely that is hurrying things unnecessarily?"

"Not if we want to prevent Edmund from borrowing even more money on his chances of fathering the future Duke, and Lottie from making it very clear that she is now a member, and a very important one, of our family."

He looked at the Marquis as he spoke, and the latter, as a man, was well aware of the way in which Lottie would behave now that she was Edmund's wife.

She had always been one of the most flamboyant women of the Town, and was to be found, when she was not performing in some sleazy Theatre or a private party, at every noisy Dance-Hall, surrounded by the most dissolute and debauched members of the aristocracy.

That she had managed to get married to anybody was a feather in her cap, and as the wife of the heir presumptive to the Duke of Buckhurst she would use her position to make herself even more notorious than she was already.

"You are right," the Marquis said. "If you have to marry, the sooner the better! I am sure that Elizabeth and Margaret can find you somebody suitable with the greatest of ease."

"Very well," the Duke replied. "Arrange everything for the second of June, and I suggest that you put the announcement in *The Gazette* as quickly as possible. That should at least keep Lottie quiet for the moment."

"I am sure you are right, dearest," Elizabeth said, "but it is not the way I would have wished you to be married."

She gave almost a little sob. Then she said:

"You are so handsome and so talented, and what is more, despite all the things that are said about you, which as you well know is your own fault, you are still a great gentleman, and I am very, very proud of you."

"So am I!" Margaret said quickly, determined not to be left out.

"Let us hope my wife can be proud of me too," the Duke said, and now there was not only a note of cynicism in his voice but also something bitter. "I daresay once we are married we can come to some

15

equable arrangement which need not concern you at the moment."

Elizabeth walked to stand beside him.

"I have prayed, Buck," she said in a low voice, "that you would find somebody to love and who would love you. Perhaps, if we are lucky, Margaret and I will find exactly the wife that every man dreams of."

The Duke laughed.

"You are a romantic, Elizabeth, and that is the sort of thing that happens only in fairy-stories! I assure you I am very happy with my life as it is, and although a wife will undoubtedly prove somewhat of an encumbrance, I will of course treat her with respect and will perform what public duties are necessary. But as far as I am concerned, she will not encroach on my private life."

There was a hard note in his voice that his sister did not miss, and she said with a sob:

"You were such an adorable little boy, and we loved you so much. What has happened that you have become so cynical and mock at everything that is beautiful and, as you say, romantic?"

"I have grown older and wiser," the Duke replied, "but do not worry about me, Elizabeth. I am very happy as I am, only infuriated that Edmund has forced me into taking a step I have avoided for a very long time."

"I am sure when you do take it," Elizabeth said, "it will not be as bad as you think."

"I hope not, but I am definitely expecting the worst," the Duke replied.

"What is that?" asked Margaret, who always had to have everything explained to her in words of one syllable.

"Boredom!" her brother answered. "The boredom of sitting looking at the same face day after day, year after year, and hearing the same banal, asinine remarks that I heard yesterday, and the day before that!"

He paused, and added as if he was working it out for himself:

"The only pleasure I will get out of such a situation is having a son whom I can teach to shoot and ride, and who will one day take my place as head of the family."

"But suppose you have daughters?" Margaret asked ingenuously.

"Then I shall undoubtedly drown them!" the Duke answered, and waited for the scream of protest that came from both his sisters' lips.

Only when the family had left him and he was alone did he ask himself almost despairingly what he had let himself in for.

After all the years of hating the idea of marriage, of considering it the end of privacy and freedom, it appalled him that he had been caught in such a fashion by a cousin he loathed the very sight of and despised.

"Damn him! He has had his revenge!" the Duke told himself, and he knew that if Edmund were aware of what he was feeling now it would give him the utmost satisfaction.

Then, as if he could not bear to think of the future and what lay ahead of him, he called for a Phaeton.

As he drove away in the direction of St. John's Wood, where he had recently installed in a house he owned an alluring and very attractive little French dancer, he thought the only way he could forget for a time was in the passion of her kisses and the fire she would undoubtedly ignite in him.

But as he approached the house on which he had spent a considerable amount of money, and even more on the horses and jewels she had extracted from him, he found himself saying beneath his breath:

"Damn all women!"

* * *

Several hours later, as the Duke returned home, he was thinking of a very attractive woman who had only recently engaged his interest.

The wife of a Diplomat, she had not long been in London, and there was no doubt that when she and the

Duke had first met a spark had flared between them which told him all too clearly what the end of the encounter would be.

When he thought of her now, he wondered if he was making a mistake in embarking on another *affaire de coeur* just before his marriage would be announced.

He did not deceive himself into thinking that his new interest would escape the notice of the tittle-tattlers and of those who followed every move he made like hawks hovering ceaselessly over his head.

She had invited him to a dinner-party, which the Duke was quite certain would consist of only two people, the dinner being served in her private Sitting-Room, which would be redolent of flowers, the perfume of which would be as heady as the wine which he would be served.

They would duel with each other with words across the table and there would be a *double entendre* in almost everything they said.

Then when dinner was over there would be the flowers, the cushion-covered sofa, and the door ajar into a candle-lit bedroom.

It was all so familiar, so much a regular part of his life, that he thought it was as normal as coming down to breakfast in his own house, or riding across the Park on one of his own horses.

Then as if the question presented itself for the first time he asked:

"What else is there?" and did not know the answer.

As he was dressing, putting on the long, slim drain-pipe trousers which had been introduced by the King when he was Prince Regent, and the long-tailed, cut-away coat, and a cravat frilled and starched, the points high above his chin-line, the Duke was thinking about himself.

When he had finished dressing, he suddenly made one of the quick decisions which only those who knew him well were aware he could do.

"Send Mr. Dalton to me," he said to his valet.

"Yes, Your Grace."

The valet hurried away, and the Duke stood looking at himself in the mirror, thinking as he did so that the lines on his face were more pronounced than they had been last year and the year before that.

"I am getting old," he told himself. "Perhaps the family is right and it is time I settled down."

Then he thought of the gauche, ignorant, rather stupid girl he would have to marry, but who would undoubtedly be exactly the right choice because her blood matched his and her father had a title the equal of his own.

She would be his wife and would expect him to perform his duty as a husband. Then she would produce the sons who were so essential to the inheritance.

Yet, she would still be sitting eternally in his house, in his life, doubtless with even less to say to him than when they were first married.

"I cannot bear it! I cannot do it!" the Duke said, and saw his lips in the mirror mouth the words.

Then as he looked he saw not his own face but Lottie's—her inviting red lips, heavily mascaraed eyes —heard the words of the bawdy songs she sang, and knew he had no alternative.

He owed it to the family and to himself to behave honourably and decently, however hard it might be.

As he thought of it he knew he was right in thinking that if he was going to marry in haste and prevent Lottie from making capital out of marrying Edmund, he must not start another scandal at this particular moment.

The door opened and Mr. Dalton came in.

He had been secretary and Comptroller to the Duke for many years, and the fact that all his houses and Estates ran on greased wheels was due to Dalton's highly skilled management and knowledge of everything that went on.

The Duke turned from the mirror.

"Send a message, Dalton, to the Baroness von Schlüter," he said, "that I unfortunately must cancel my engagement with her this evening, owing to the fact that His Majesty requires my presence at Buckingham Palace."

"Very good, Your Grace," Mr. Dalton replied in an impassive tone.

"Tomorrow, send her a large basket of flowers in the usual way."

"Very good, Your Grace."

"I am leaving for Newmarket in the morning," the Duke added, "and as I shall be staying for longer than I usually do, I think it would be best if you came with me."

"Of course, Your Grace."

The Duke sighed.

"Now, Dalton, where shall I go tonight? I cannot bear to stay here thinking about myself."

"Of course not, Your Grace."

"I am asking you where I can find amusement and forgetfulness of what lies ahead."

The Duke spoke with a violence which made his Comptroller look at him speculatively, but he never asked unnecessary questions.

"I suggest Your Grace go first to White's," he said, "where you will undoubtedly find a number of Your Grace's friends. I am sure they will have many suggestions as to where the most amusing evening can be found."

"You are right, Dalton," the Duke said. "That is exactly what I will do, but if I do go on elsewhere, it is problematical whether at the moment I will find anything amusing."

Mr. Dalton still said nothing, and as if the Duke knew only too well what he was thinking, he said sharply:

"I am to be married, Dalton! Does that surprise you? It happens to be the truth."

"I rather suspected that might happen, Your Grace, after we learnt of Mr. Edmund's marriage."

The Duke stared at his Comptroller for a moment. Then he laughed.

"Really, Dalton! Is there nothing you do not know? I was anticipating that for once I might be a jump ahead of you."

"Mr. Edmund's marriage was announced this morning in *The Gazette*," Mr. Dalton said quietly. "I had intended to show the announcement to Your Grace when you returned, but I felt quite sure that was why Your Grace's family had called and were waiting for you."

"You were right, Dalton, quite right," the Duke agreed. "And as they made clear to me, I have no alternative but to take a wife, and that is what I intend to do."

"I can only hope, Your Grace," Mr. Dalton said slowly, "that a wife will make you happy."

"She will make me damned unhappy!" the Duke retorted. "Nobody knows that better than you! But I suppose, if there is to be a lamb to the slaughter, it has to be me! God, what a fate! And do not dare to give me your good wishes!"

He did not wait for his Comptroller's reply, but walked out of the room, making a tremendous effort at self-control in not slamming the door behind him.

Chapter Two

$\mathcal{L}$ ady Samala Wynn rode into the stables, avoiding the pot-holes in the cobbled yard dexterously, after long familiarity with them.

She dismounted and led her horse into a stable which had originally been built to hold forty horses but now contained only three.

In the nearest stall the roof let in the rain, and she therefore put *Mercury* into the next stall, which at least was still weather-proof.

As she undid the girths and removed the saddle, an ancient groom came slowly down the passageway to say:

"Did ye 'ave a good ride, M'Lady?"

"Yes, thank you, Walters, but so much young grass is bad for *Mercury*. I think you had better give him a feed of oats this evening."

"T'ain't possible, M'Lady."

"Why?"

"Mr. Turner won't supply us wi' no more, 'til us 'ave paid 'is bill."

Samala made an exclamation, but she did not protest, knowing that it was what she might have expected.

"Well, give him plenty of hay," she said, "but it is not the same, as we both know."

"No, M'Lady, but there's nothin' us c'n do about it."

22

"Nothing," Samala agreed.

She hung up the bridle inside the stall and carried the ancient side-saddle outside to put it on a hook on the wall.

The spring sunshine coming through the window where most of the panes of glass were broken turned her hair to gold, but her blue eyes were worried as she walked away from the stables, again picking her way carefully over the holes in the yard.

As she walked she was thinking how critical things were becoming, and was wondering if there was anything left in the house to sell.

She was well aware that she and her father must often go hungry, but she could not bear the horses to suffer, and she wondered desperately, as she had done so often before, where they could find some money to meet their debts.

Anybody looking at the outside of the Earl of Kenwyn's beautiful Elizabethan house would find it hard to understand the battle that was being fought inside against poverty, privation, and the damage which came from years of neglect, until at times Samala thought the whole house would crumble to the ground about their ears.

And yet at the same time, because it meant so much to her father, she knew that she could not suggest the obvious solution: that they should move into one of the smaller houses or even a cottage on the Estate.

He had said to her once, and she had never forgotten it:

"If I have to drown I will go down with my ship, with my colours flying! I will not surrender to anybody —God, man, or these damned debts!"

It was his pride, Samala thought, that made him speak like that. And she had inherited it and knew that she too would fight and go on fighting.

Perhaps they would die of starvation and their bodies would be left unburied on the ancient wooden floors that had been laid down in the reign of Queen Elizabeth.

Then, because she was young and the sun was shining, she told herself that things could not be as bad as all that and somehow they would survive, although she could not for the moment think how.

She rounded the corner of the house, and as she did so she saw in astonishment that outside the front door was a very impressive, luxurious-looking carriage drawn by four horses with a coachman and a footman on the box.

Samala wondered who could be calling on her father and instantly hoped it was not one of the neighbours in the County, asking him to undertake yet another duty which invariably cost money.

As her father was so respected and everybody loved him, he was continually being approached to be the Chairman of this project or the Patron of another.

While he hated not to take his rightful place in County affairs, he knew, as Samala did, that every such position meant that he must contribute either money if it was a Charity, or hospitality if it was a Committee.

Sometimes they could get away with a meeting, which involved providing the guests with no more than a glass of sherry, but even sherry cost money, and the cellar at Kenwyn Priory, which had once been famous, was now empty, except for some stone kegs and barrels that had stood there for centuries.

As Samala reached the carriage she looked quickly at the coat-of-arms on the panel, thinking that if it was familiar it would tell her to whom it belonged.

But the design of a rampant Griffon was unknown to her, and she quickly mounted the steps, thinking that she must support her father and help him to refuse whatever was being suggested, without revealing the true reason for it.

Then as she crossed the Hall she wondered if in her old, threadbare habit she looked too untidy to greet visitors, and was well aware that if they were people of importance they would think it strange that she was not wearing a riding-hat.

Because hers was very old and dilapidated, it was so much more comfortable to slip her long fair hair into a chignon and forget the conventions.

Then she told herself with a smile that it was unlikely that anybody would take any notice of her appearance, and she was quite certain that her father would want her with him.

She opened the door of the Study, which was the room they used, the Drawing-Rooms being shut up and the Library being too big and cold, except during the warmth of summer.

Samala had made the Study as comfortable as possible, bringing in the pieces of furniture which she and her father liked the best, and the paintings which they loved and which, being entailed, could not be sold.

As she entered the room she expected to find a gentleman in one of the comfortable but shabby leather armchairs. Instead, to her astonishment, there was a lady, and a very elegant and beautiful one at that.

As she tried to prevent herself from looking too surprised, her father, who had his back to her, turned round, and she knew he was relieved to see her and at the same time something was perturbing him.

"I am sorry to be late, Papa," she said, advancing towards the fireplace, "but it was such a lovely day, and I only wish you had been riding with me."

"I wish I had," the Earl replied a little heavily.

As Samala reached his side, he looked at the lady sitting opposite him and said:

"May I present my daughter, Samala? This, Samala, is the Marchioness of Hull. She has come here with a very strange proposition, but I want you to listen to it."

"Yes, of course, Papa," Samala answered, and going up to the Marchioness she curtseyed and held out her hand.

She thought that the older woman looked at her scrutinisingly, in a somewhat embarrassing fashion, but she was intent on noting the elegance of her fashionable, high-brimmed bonnet with its edging of lace and small ostrich feathers trimming it, which were blue to match the Marchioness's silk gown.

Then to Samala's astonishment she said:

"You are very lovely child, in fact, far more beautiful than I had dared to hope."

It seemed a strange thing to say, and Samala looked at her questioningly, then at her father, and because she knew him so well, she realised that he felt embarrassed.

He rose from the chair in which he had been sitting to stand with his back to the empty fireplace.

"The Marchioness, Samala," he began, and he appeared to be choosing his words with care, "has come here on behalf of her brother, to ask if I will give him your hand in marriage!"

If her father had dropped a bomb at her feet Samala could not have been more astonished.

Then she thought it must be a joke, but there was no doubt that her father was being very serious, and with an effort she managed to say:

"This is a great . . . surprise, Papa!"

"I knew you would think so," the Earl replied. "At the same time, it is certainly a marriage such as I would wish for you, and which is, in a way, a great honour."

"Have you met the gentleman in question?" Samala asked, knowing that what she really wanted to learn was whether she had met him herself.

The Earl shook his head.

"No, I do not think we have ever met," he said, "but I should appear very ignorant of the Sporting World if I were not aware that His Grace's horses have won all the Classic Races."

"Of course," the Marchioness said, "my brother is a great sportsman and an outstanding rider, which, as your daughter obviously loves riding, should be an interest in common."

She spoke eagerly, almost as if, Samala thought, she was trying to entice her, and she continued:

"In fact, it is only fair to say that my brother's horses, not only those he races but those he rides, are superlative, and I think, Lady Samala, you will find yourself entranced by them as I have always been."

Samala thought that it was a strange conversation and it was astonishing to talk so much about horses when she should be speaking about the man who wished to marry her.

In a small voice that somehow seemed unlike her own she asked:

"Surely there will be a chance for me to meet the gentleman who wishes to marry me? Then we can talk about the things which are of mutual interest."

The Marchioness appeared to hesitate, and the Earl said almost sharply:

"Her Ladyship has been explaining to me, Samala, that it is imperative, although I cannot quite understand why, that your marriage should take place on the second of June."

"But, Papa . . . that is less than three weeks away."

"Yes, I know," the Earl said, "and it seems to me strange, very strange."

"I have already explained," the Marchioness interposed, "that my brother wishes to be married before Royal Ascot. He has several horses running and hopes this year to win the Gold Cup."

"I should have thought," the Earl said quietly, "that on this occasion, His Grace's marriage should take priority over everything else."

Samala looked from one to the other of them in bewilderment. Then the Marchioness, leaning forward in her chair, addressed her.

"Please, dear," she said, "or may I call you Samala? Try to understand that my brother is a somewhat

27

unpredictable person, even though I love him and find him a very fascinating character. He has made up his mind that he wishes to be married on the second of June, and I do beg you to agree to his proposition."

She must have thought that Samala's expression was one of doubt, because she said:

"Surely you can understand what this will mean to you? You will be the Chatelaine of one of the finest houses in England, besides other houses that my brother owns; you will have clothes, gowns which will make you, I know, the *Belle* of every Ball you attend, and jewels that are unsurpassed by any other collection in the whole country."

She paused, then as if she could not help herself, she glanced round the room at the threadbare carpet, the faded curtains, and the furniture, which all needed re-covering.

"Surely," she said, "you must understand how much this will change your life, almost as if your Fairy-Godmother had waved a magic wand or you had walked into a dream."

"I do understand what you are saying to me," Samala replied, "but before I decide, I would like to meet . . . the man I am to . . . marry and be quite certain I would make him . . . happy."

There was a little pause before the Marchioness said:

"That is what I have been explaining to your father. Unfortunately, my brother has had to go away, and he will be returning only a day or so before the wedding."

Samala stared at her in astonishment.

"Are you really suggesting, My Lady, that I should marry somebody I have never seen or spoken to? It is impossible."

As she spoke she turned and went to stand by her father, slipping her arm through his as if she must hold on to him for security and protection.

He put his hand over hers as if he understood what she was feeling.

"I agree it is a very strange proposition indeed, Samala. At the same time, as the Marchioness has said, as the Duchess of Buckhurst you will have a position which is without parallel."

As he spoke Samala stiffened and looked up at him.

"Did you say . . . the Duchess of . . . Buckhurst, Papa?"

"I thought I had explained," the Marchioness interrupted, "but perhaps it was before you arrived, that my brother is the Duke of Buckhurst."

"Are you sure?" Samala enquired.

The Marchioness smiled.

"Of course I am sure! If you have heard of him, which I am sure you have with your interest in horses, you will know I have not exaggerated his position in the Sporting World, besides his importance as a friend of the King, and he is one of the most important Dukes in Great Britain."

Samala was not listening.

"The Duke of Buckhurst!" she said under her breath.

Then she looked up at her father.

"Although, Papa, as I have said it seems a very strange proposition, I am prepared, if he . . . wishes to marry me, to . . . accept the Duke."

Before the Earl could speak, the Marchioness gave a little cry of delight.

"I am so glad you have said that! What a sensible child you are! I know how delighted my brother will be when I write and tell him that you have agreed."

As if he must assert himself, the Earl said:

"My daughter must be married from here, of course, as it is our home."

The Marchioness drew in her breath.

"I think, My Lord, that would be a mistake. You can understand that the tenants at Buckhurst Park will be

very disappointed if they are not to be part of the
festivities. My husband has already arranged for a huge
marquee to be erected, where they will be entertained
with barrels of beer and cider, and so much to eat that it
makes me feel quite ill to think of it!"

She smiled before she went on:

"Our other guests of course will be entertained in
the Ball-Room with every possible delicacy. And a cake
is being baked by our own Chefs and it would break their
hearts if it was cooked by anybody else."

Samala pressed her father's arm, and he knew she
was thinking it would be with the greatest difficulty that
they could provide a plain sponge-cake at the moment,
let alone anything elaborate.

It would be quite impossible for him to provide food
and champagne such as the guests at the wedding of the
Duke of Buckhurst would expect automatically.

"Very well, I must concede your point," the Earl
said, "and fortunately we are not too far away from
Buckhurst Park. In fact, I should think Samala and I
could do the journey in about two-and-a-half hours."

The Marchioness laughed.

"It depends, My Lord, very much on what horses
you have! It took me only an hour-and-a-half to get here
today, and I am sure for the wedding my brother will
send one of his famous teams and a carriage which is so
well sprung that you will feel you are riding on clouds
rather than on a rough road."

She paused, then looking at Samala said:

"There is of course one thing on which I will insist,
and that is that my wedding-present to you, dear, will be
your trousseau. I am afraid some of the gowns will not be
finished until after the wedding has taken place, but at
least I promise you you will have enough to start your
honeymoon looking beautiful."

"Thank you very much."

Samala knew as she spoke that her father was rigid,

as if he felt it was insulting to insinuate that he could not provide a trousseau for his own daughter.

At the same time, she was well aware that they had not the money to buy one gown, let alone a whole trousseau.

"Now let us be practical," the Marchioness said. "If you will give me your measurements, or better still an old gown which fits you, I will send it to London and arrange for Madame Bertin, who is by far the smartest dressmaker in Bond Street, to have half-a-dozen ready for you. Then she will come here to you to choose from the sketches and the patterns she will provide, and she will bring what else you require."

"It is very kind of you, My Lady."

"I want to be kind, very kind to my new sister-in-law," the Marchioness answered, "and I cannot tell you how happy I am that my brother will have such a beautiful and charming wife who belongs to a family which I know is as proud of its antecedents as we are."

She rose to her feet as she spoke and held out her hand to the Earl.

"Thank you, My Lord," she said. "I know we shall see a lot of each other in the future, and my husband, who says he has met you, will look forward to entertaining you at our house in London, and we hope too that you will stay with us in the country."

"Thank you," the Earl replied.

The Marchioness turned to Samala.

"Good-bye, my dear. I know you will never regret accepting my brother as a husband, and remember that all I want to do is to help you. My sister, Lady Bredon, will say the same thing. We love Buck and have prayed for his happiness, which I am sure you will somehow contrive to give him."

There was a strange note in her voice, Samala thought, almost as if she was hoping against hope that what she was saying would come true.

Then she kissed her, and as she walked towards the door her father hurried to open it for her.

Samala did not accompany them across the Hall to where the Marchioness's carriage was waiting outside.

Instead, she stood very still in the Study, her hands clasped together, her eyes looking ahead as if she was seeing not the paintings on the wall but something very different.

"The Duke of Buckhurst!" she whispered to herself.

Although her voice was barely audible, she felt as if it rang out round the four walls and touched the ceiling.

* * *

Driving away, the Marchioness of Hull gave a deep sigh and thought that, incredible though it seemed, her quest was at an end.

It was only when she and her sister had made out a list of eligible girls from aristocratic families whom they could welcome as Buck's wife that they realised they had been over-optimistic in thinking that anybody they invited to marry him would jump at the opportunity.

One after another the fathers of the girls on the list had firmly turned down the proposition without even giving them a chance to discuss it.

The Duke of Dorset was extremely blunt.

"I am not such a fool," he said acidly, "as not to be aware that to be the Duchess of Buckhurst has great social advantages, but as I am extremely fond of my daughter, I wish her to have at least a sporting chance of happiness in any marriage I arrange for her."

The Marchioness had been unable to answer this, and he had added:

"I like Buck, he amuses me, and his horses always beat mine, but I cannot envisage a worse hell for any woman than to be married to him. I do not believe for one moment that simply because he has been forced into marriage he will change his ways and become a reformed character."

He spoke sarcastically, and every father had said much the same thing.

They were all aware of the reason for the Duke's precipitate marriage, and the Marchioness and her husband were well aware that nothing they could say could gloss over the fact that he was taking a wife only because their cousin Edmund had married Lott Linkley.

The Marquis also had the uncomfortable feeling that none of the families whom they approached were amused by the fact that for the first time in his life Buckhurst was having to do something he disliked, and was not getting his own way as he always had ever since they had known him.

He knew that Elizabeth and Margaret were beginning to despair as their list of eligible young girls grew shorter and shorter, until they were finally left with the Earl of Kenwyn's daughter, and with the anxious knowledge that time was running out.

"I will drive over to the Priory tomorrow afternoon," the Marchioness said, "but if the Earl refuses to entertain the idea, I cannot imagine where we can go next."

"Kenwyn is miserably poor," the Marquis replied. "His house is falling in ruins about him, and I have heard that he refuses all invitations in the County because he will not accept hospitality which he cannot return."

"It sounds a very honourable way of behaving," the Marchioness observed.

"He is an honourable man," her husband agreed. "He has always been exceedingly proud, and I doubt if he will agree to Buck's proposition that the marriage should take place on the second of June."

"Why must he always make things so difficult?" Margaret asked plaintively.

"Buck is used to getting his own way," Elizabeth replied, "and he will never understand that none of all these families have any wish for their daughters to become the Duchess of Buckhurst if that includes having Buck as a husband."

Margaret gave a little cry of horror.

"If Buck heard you say that he would have a stroke!"

"But it is true," her sister replied. "Quite frankly, if the Earl refuses, he really is our last hope. We shall have to start all over again, and it will be quite impossible to do it in the time."

"Well, you tell Buck I am not going to try any more," Margaret said sharply.

"Nor am I," the Marquis said.

Elizabeth sighed.

"I can only pray that since the Earl of Kenwyn is so poor he will realise the advantages there would be not only for his daughter but for himself to have Buck as a son-in-law."

She smiled as she added:

"If there is one thing on which we all agree, it is that, although Buck may have his faults, he is extremely generous, and I cannot believe, however much he dislikes having a wife, he would allow his father-in-law to have to skimp and save and be as poor as a Church-mouse."

"Then for goodness' sake," Margaret said, "make that clear to the Earl."

Before Samala came into the room, the Marchioness had thought that however persuasive she was being, she had failed.

She had realised that her husband had been right when he had said that the Earl of Kenwyn was proud, and when she had said the marriage was to take place on the second of June, she saw that his chin went up as if he regarded such haste as an insult.

She thought too that Samala would understand-ably insist on seeing the man she was to marry, and she would therefore have to go back and admit defeat.

Then, amazingly, the girl, when she learnt who her suitor was, had accepted him without any more to-do.

'Perhaps it is the glamour of racing, or perhaps she has heard of how handsome Buck is,' the Marchioness thought.

Whatever the explanation, she had succeeded and now for the moment their troubles were over, although she was half-afraid Samala might back out at the last moment.

"The whole proposition is ridiculous!" she said to herself as she had said ever since Buck had set down the conditions for his marriage.

At any rate, it was a relief to know that they did not have to go on listening to the truth about Buck, and indeed she felt as if she had reached the top of a high mountain when she had thought that its peak was beyond her reach.

* * *

The Earl walked back from the front door to the Study, intending to ask Samala for an explanation as to why she had accepted the Duke of Buckhurst without any further deliberation.

"I want her to be happy," he said to himself, but he knew when she was gone he would miss her desperately and the empty, poverty-stricken house would be intolerable without her.

"The whole thing is ridiculous!" he told himself. "I shall tell her to refuse the man, and we will go on as we are."

Because he lived out of the Social World, the Earl knew very little about the Duke, apart from his sporting success, and the tales of his indiscretions and his raffish reputation had not percolated to the Priory.

In fact, as the Earl disliked gossip of any sort and he actually saw very few people, he had no idea that the Duke's name was a by-word and his love-affairs were the talk of London.

All the same, he still thought it very strange that Samala should be immediately willing to marry him, although he knew that from a worldly point of view it would ensure that she was safe and protected for the rest of her life.

"But will that make her happy?" he asked.

He was determined to ask her that question, but when he entered the Study he found she was not there.

* * *

The Duke received the letter sent by a groom to his house in Newmarket telling him that his bride was to be the Earl of Kenwyn's daughter and her name was Samala.

He read what his sister had written, and noted with a cynical twist to his lips that she had added:

> *Samala is very pretty, in fact I think the right word is "lovely," and she will certainly grace the Buckhurst diamonds.*
>
> *As I expect you know, the Wynn family is as old and as distinguished as ours. The Earl is good-looking and has a delightful manner, but they are very, very poor.*
>
> *The house is beautiful from the outside, but very poverty-stricken within, and there appeared to be no servants. I had the feeling that most of the rooms were shut up.*
>
> *The garden is uncared for and the drive pot-holed, but Samala is like a lily amidst such dilapidation, and I do not think you will be disappointed. . . .*

The Duke could hardly bother to read to the end of the letter, but pushed it into a drawer and went from the room to find that one unexpected guest had arrived uninvited.

If he had decided that he had no wish to start a love-affair on the eve of his marriage, the Baroness von Schlüter had very different ideas.

He had no sooner arrived in Newmarket and installed himself in his very large and impressive house to welcome the house-party, which would arrive the next day and which consisted mostly of men, when the Butler came to tell him that there was a lady to see him.

"A lady?" the Duke enquired. "Who is it?"

"She did not give her name, Your Grace. She only said that it was of the utmost importance that she should see you at once."

The Duke looked impatiently at the clock.

He had been just about to go upstairs to dress for dinner, and if there was one thing he disliked it was having to hurry over his bath and, even more, to be late for a meal.

He thought he might tell the lady, whoever she might be, to go away and come back again tomorrow. Then he thought that would be even more irritating.

He therefore walked rather disagreeably into the Morning-Room, where the Butler had left his unknown visitor.

Then as he opened the door he saw who was there and that she was extremely lovely and seductive in a manner which had intrigued him at their first meeting.

"This is a surprise!" he said as he walked across the room.

She held out her hand, and as he kissed it perfunctorily the Baroness said:

"I have come to throw myself on your mercy. I arrived in Newmarket to find that the rooms I had booked at the Hotel have, through some mistake, not been kept for me, and unless I sleep on the Downs, I have nowhere to lay my head."

The Duke did not believe a word of it. At the same time, the way she spoke was very enticing, and her broken accent fascinated him.

"You are alone?" he asked.

"My husband may join me later," she replied, "but some important Politicians have just arrived from Paris, and he could not leave London."

Again the Duke was quite certain that this was untrue, but there was no point in saying so.

"Please, *mon cher*," the Baroness pleaded, looking at him under her eye-lashes, "let me stay here with you tonight, and perhaps tomorrow I shall be able to find other accommodation."

There was therefore nothing the Duke could do but instal her in one of the many comfortable and empty rooms in his house.

She not only sparkled like a twinkling star at dinner, but made it very clear as the evening ended what she expected from him.

Because he found her very attractive, and because the principles which had made him cancel their dinner together the night before seemed now rather farfetched and unnecessary, the Duke had succumbed, as he had always done all his life, to his own desires.

He found that she was, as he had expected, both passionate and exciting, and the spark they had seen in each other's eyes the first time they met became a raging fire from which it was impossible to escape.

There was no question of the Baroness leaving the next day or the next.

When the racing ended at Newmarket, as the Duke had no wish to return to London, to hear his friends talking about his forthcoming marriage and gloating over his discomfiture, he had taken her to one of his other houses, a very delightful Hunting-Lodge in Leicestershire.

While he was there he really did not think very much about his marriage, and when the Marchioness wrote to tell him that the Earl of Kenwyn's daughter would be his wife, he merely thought that everything was going as planned.

This at any rate would stop Edmund from borrowing on his chance of becoming the Duke, and Lottie's unborn child would cease to have any particular importance.

He allowed himself to forget everything but the allurement and the fascinating accent of the Baroness and the fire that leapt higher and higher when they touched each other.

* * *

Exactly a week after the Marchioness had called at Kenwyn Priory, Madame Bertin arrived in a Post Chaise with a pile of boxes containing gowns which made Samala gasp when she saw them.

It was so long since she had had a new gown, or even seen the pictures in the *Ladies' Journal*, that she really had no idea what the fashion was, although she had thought that if she had anything as lovely as what the Marchioness was wearing, she would be very happy.

But Elizabeth Hull, who had been a beauty, was well aware that clothes were very important, and besides, at the back of her mind she thought that perhaps, despite her brother's avowed antagonism to marriage, he might eventually come to love his own wife.

Her brain told her that this was very unlikely. At the same time, she was a romantic at heart, and although Margaret laughed at her and her husband usually failed to understand what she was talking about, she wanted to believe that, as in the fairy-tales, Prince Charming lived happily ever afterwards.

She knew that her brother's love-affairs, if that was the right word for them, had always been with sophisticated, exquisitely dressed beauties who used every known artifice to make them shine like a crystal chandelier and sparkle like fireworks.

She also realised that Samala's halo of gold hair, her blue eyes, and her very young, almost child-like face had beauty that was unusual, but she had the uncomfortable feeling that her brother would not appreciate it.

At first she had been so thrilled and delighted that Samala had accepted the amazing proposition of being married in under three weeks, that she had not really thought very much about the bride but only of the bridegroom.

Now, because she was a kind woman and was very

much aware of how difficult Buck could be, she set out to make Samala into a beauty and to enhance the qualities which were essentially hers.

They were, she knew, very different from those of the woman with whom her brother, she had been informed, was currently amusing himself.

It was not surprising that the Baroness had followed her brother to Newmarket and that he had taken her from Newmarket to Leicestershire.

The Marchioness had seen the Baroness, and she knew that her dark hair, flashing eyes, and sensuous, voluptuous body were very much in Buck's taste, where Samala was in every way the exact opposite.

Because Margaret wanted to meet her, the Marchioness, her sister, and her husband drove to the Priory two days after her first visit, and found Samala arranging flowers in the Study.

She was quite unselfconscious and unperturbed by their arrival, greeting them politely and, the Marchioness thought, with a grace that was somewhat unusual in so young a girl.

It did not seem to worry her that she was wearing a very old cotton gown that had been washed until the colour had left it, and that she had grown out of it until it was too tight over her breasts.

Her hair was arranged casually in a chignon because she had been riding, and both the Marchioness and Lady Bredon appreciated that she made no apology for herself or the house, and only hurried to the kitchen to make tea and bring it to them on a tray.

"I am afraid there are no cakes or biscuits," she said, "but if you would like some sandwiches, I can pick a cucumber from the garden."

"No, we are not hungry," the Marchioness said quickly, "only a little thirsty after the journey, and this tea is delicious."

As she spoke, she knew it was the very cheapest tea available, and Samala gave a little smile to show she appreciated her tact, and pretended not to notice that Lady Bredon, having sipped from her cup, put it down and did not touch it again.

They talked for a little while. Then the Earl came in and seemed surprised to see them.

The Marquis, however, greeted him effusively and they were soon talking about horses and the difficulties the farmers were having in the country, and they obviously had no wish to include the ladies in their conversation.

"Some of your gowns will be here the day after tomorrow," the Marchioness said, "and I wonder, dear child, if you would like me to come over and help you to choose from the sketches which Madame Bertin is bringing you."

"I would love you to do that, if it is no trouble," Samala answered. "At the same time, please, you must not be too . . . extravagant and give me . . . too many lovely things."

She lowered her voice as she added:

"It is rather . . . embarrassing for Papa to feel he cannot provide me with my trousseau."

"I thought you would feel like that," the Marchioness said, "but if you had been somebody rich I would have bought a large diamond brooch or perhaps a necklace for my future sister-in-law. But I knew you would consider it much more practical to have pretty gowns and all the accessories to go with them."

Samala laughed.

"Much more practical," she said. "I cannot imagine that anybody would be very impressed if I were wearing a diamond brooch or a sparkling necklace with this gown!"

Because she was so unselfconscious and her laughter seemed to ring out in the sunshine, both the Marchioness and Margaret Bredon were entranced by her.

Going home, Lady Bredon said:

"She is lovely, and I think we are very fortunate to have found exactly the right wife for Buck, and somebody who will undoubtedly make him a very good Duchess."

"I only hope Buck thinks so!" the Marquis remarked.

Then there was silence while all three were thinking that Buck would have very little in common with the country girl who had never had a pretty gown until now, and who knew nothing of the world in which he shone so brilliantly and at the same time so devastatingly.

"Is that woman still with him?" Margaret asked in a low voice.

The Marquis nodded.

"I heard from one of my friends this morning, and he told me he had dined with Buck the night before last. She was there, and the life and soul of the party."

They looked at one another in dismay, then as if there was nothing more to say they drove on in silence.

Chapter Three

Coming back from riding with her father, Samala thought how happy they always were when they were together.

They had had a long ride and had talked a great deal about the Estate, about their difficulties over the old people whose houses needed repairing, and about the School in the village, which was very inadequate and, as the Earl had said despairingly, required a new teacher.

"If I could afford to provide a decent one, at least for the children of those I employ," he said, "I would feel I was doing my duty for the next generation."

It was typical of him, Samala thought, that he was always thinking of other people rather than of himself, and she knew that her mother had been the same.

"If only Papa had even a little money to spend," she whispered as they put their horses in the dilapidated stables and saw that they had hay and water.

Walters was so old that all he could do was to clean up the stalls and, when his rheumatism was not too bad, groom the horses.

Otherwise, it meant that the Earl and Samala had to do everything themselves, and although neither of them minded, Samala often thought there were far more important things her father should be engaged on and he was wasting his brain.

43

Only she knew how intelligent he was, and how when they talked together at meal-times and could forget their immediate problems, their minds would range over subjects which embraced the whole Universe.

She knew that however poor and shabby she might be, nobody would be able to say that she was not in fact well educated.

When her father and mother could afford it she had always had good teachers on every important subject, and when that became impossible they had taught her themselves.

Her father had gained his degree at Oxford, and, what was more important, he was an avid reader, as her mother had been.

Ever since she had been a tiny child Samala could remember that there had been spirited arguments at meal-times on all sorts of subjects from Oriental Religions to Political Economics, and she had never been allowed to feel that she was too young to join in.

Now as she took off her riding-habit and put on one of her old cotton gowns, she found herself wondering who her father would talk to if she was not there.

So much had happened since the Marchioness had called so unexpectedly with her fantastic proposition that Samala felt that she had forgotten that while her own life would change, her father's life would remain the same.

Except, of course, that it would be solitary, and he would be alone in what already seemed sometimes like a ghost-house.

"What can I do about him? What can I do?" she asked.

Then suddenly, almost as if a voice were prompting her, she knew the answer to her problem.

After they had had luncheon, which consisted as usual of pigeon, because there was very little else at this time of the year which could be shot in the Park, Samala asked tentatively:

"What are you planning to do this afternoon, Papa?"

The Earl sighed.

"I am going through the Farm accounts and the rents with Mr. Owen from the Bank. As it will be a very dreary meeting and undoubtedly most depressing, I suggest you do not join us."

"I would much rather not, Papa," Samala answered, "and I am sure Mr. Owen will advise you as best he can."

"The only thing he could do that would be really helpful," the Earl said, "is to give me a large loan. But how can I ask for that when there is not a chance in a million of it ever being repaid?"

He spoke unusually bitterly, and Samala got up from the table, put her arms round his neck, and kissed his cheek.

"Perhaps, Papa, when we least expect it we shall find a pot of gold at the end of the rainbow. Then everything will be changed."

The Earl put his arm round her and drew her close to him.

"That is what I go on trying to believe," he said, "but my hopes are beginning to die hard, and the only thing I can be thankful for is that you at least will have everything you want in life."

Samala longed to say that she would share everything with him, but she knew that would only make him retort angrily that he was not taking charity from anybody—least of all his son-in-law.

"Somehow I shall have to help him," she told herself, "but it is going to be difficult."

When her father had gone to his Study to await the arrival of the local Bank Manager, who, because he was fond of the Earl, helped with the accounts without charging him a penny, she went upstairs.

She changed into her riding-clothes and went to the stables to saddle their third horse, who because he had not been exercised that morning was fresh and frisky.

He was by no means well bred, and Samala did not

love him as she loved *Mercury*, but he was a better carriage horse than the others and also was a stand-by in case of emergencies.

It was very much quicker for Samala to ride across country to reach her destination than if she had followed the twisting, turning lanes, which would have lengthened her journey considerably.

Instead, in just over three-quarters-of-an-hour she arrived at the small Church and turned in at some impressive gates which belonged to what was locally known as "The Big House."

It was very large, square and formidable, and, in contrast to the Priory, undoubtedly ugly.

Samala dismounted at the front door and a groom came hurrying from the stables to take her horse, and when she had climbed the steps the front door was opened and a middle-aged Butler said with a smile:

"Good-afternoon, Lady Samala, you're quite a stranger."

"Good-afternoon, White!" Samala replied. "Is Mrs. Henley at home?"

"She's not receiving, M'Lady, but I'm sure she'd like to see Your Ladyship," the Butler replied.

He led the way across a stiff, somewhat unwelcoming Hall and opened the door into a square, high-ceilinged Drawing-Room.

"Lady Samala Wynn, Ma'am!" he announced.

There was a little cry from the end of the room, where a lady was sitting in the window working at a large piece of embroidery.

She set it down and hurried towards Samala, holding out both her hands.

"Samala, what a surprise! I thought you had forgotten me."

"No, of course not," Samala answered, "but there have been so many things happening that I have had no time to come and see you, and certainly no time for writing."

"What has been happening?" Mrs. Henley asked. "Come and sit down and tell me all about it, and I am sure you would like some refreshment."

"I would not refuse some of your delicious iced coffee," Samala replied, "in fact I have been greedy enough to be thinking of it all the time I have been riding here."

Mrs. Henley laughed, and the Butler, who had been waiting in the doorway, hurried away to fetch it.

Samala sat down on the window-seat, pulling off her riding-hat as she did so, so that the sun haloed her fair hair.

"You look very pretty, dearest child," Mrs. Henley said, "and I have missed you."

"I have missed you too," Samala replied, "and I kept hoping that you would come over to see us."

Mrs. Henley looked down at the embroidery in her lap, and after a moment's pause she said:

"You and your—father always seem so—busy that I do not—like to feel I am—intruding."

Samala's eyes were on her face as she said:

"Papa misses you, too. He said once that he wondered if perhaps you had gone to London to enjoy yourself."

She saw the colour rise in Mrs. Henley's cheeks, and it encouraged her to add:

"It is actually about Papa that I have come to see you."

"About your—father?"

There was no doubt of the surprise in Mrs. Henley's voice, and now the colour in her cheeks was accentuated and made her look very much younger than her thirty-five years.

Maureen Henley was not a beauty, but she had a sweet, kind, attractive face that drew people to her like a magnet.

Samala had loved her ever since she had first known her, which was soon after she came to live in the neighbourhood as the bride of General Alexander Henley.

An avowed bachelor all his life, or rather, as he had said himself, forced to remain so because he was always on active service in some obscure part of the world, he had only married when he had retired, and the girl was very much younger than himself.

She was the daughter of a brother Officer who had died of the injuries he had received during active service.

Because she was broken-hearted by her father's death and because she was very much alone in the world, Maureen had felt she would find security and comfort in the arms of a man who was actually old enough to be her grandfather.

She had certainly made the General a very good wife, and as he had no children, when he died she had found herself with a large Estate and enough money to go anywhere and do anything she wanted.

Yet, because she had always lived so quietly, first with her wounded and crippled father, then with her elderly husband, she had no idea what to do with herself or with her money.

She had therefore devoted herself to good works in the County, and very much to the Earl's relief had taken over the management of his Orphanage which was on the boundary of the Kenwyn Estate, where it bordered the land belonging to Maureen.

At first Mrs. Henley had come to the Priory with every problem she felt she could not solve herself.

Then, strangely, as it seemed to Samala, her father began to avoid such meetings, and on two occasions when he had seen Maureen's smart carriage coming down the drive he had slipped out of the house by the garden-door and stayed away until she had left.

"Do you not want to see Mrs. Henley, Papa?" Samala had asked. "I thought you liked her."

"She is a marvellous person," the Earl had replied,

"but she should not be wasting her time on orphans, she should get married again and enjoy herself."

Samala had looked at him in surprise. Then she had said:

"Perhaps she feels she is too old."

"Too old? I have never heard such nonsense!" her father had snapped. "She is young and lovely and should not waste herself in this dead-and-alive part of the world."

He had spoken so violently, and had gone out of the room slamming the door behind him, that Samala had been amazed.

Wondering if Maureen Henley and her father had quarrelled over something, she had not pressed him for an explanation. Nor had she expressed her surprise when Mrs. Henley no longer came to the Priory.

Now, because she was older and looked at what had happened in a more intelligent way, she thought she understood, and somehow she had to put things right.

"First of all," she said, "I must tell you my news. I am to be married!"

"Married?" Maureen Henley exclaimed. "But, dearest one, that is wonderful! But to whom?"

"It seems incredible," Samala said, "but it is true! The Duke of Buckhurst has asked me to marry him."

Because she felt a little shy in making such an announcement, she did not look at Maureen Henley as she spoke and therefore she did not see the look first of incredulity in her eyes, then an expression of concern.

"The Duke of Buckhurst?" she repeated in a low voice. "Are you sure?"

"That is what I ask myself," Samala replied with a smile. "Yes, I am sure, and I am to be married on the second of June."

"But that is in a week's time!"

"Yes, I know."

"But why was I not told? Why is it a secret?"

"It is not a secret after today," Samala replied,

"because it will be in *The Gazette*, and I expect you will receive an invitation for the wedding either tomorrow or the next day. I know the Duke's sister, the Marchioness of Hull, is sending out the invitations as soon as the announcement appears in the newspapers."

As she spoke, she had no idea that the Marquis and Marchioness had held up the announcement longer than was necessary, for the simple reason that they were hoping the Duke would return to London from Leicestershire unaccompanied by the Baroness.

Because there had been no sign of him, they had felt obliged, even though they were afraid of the gossip that might arise from it, to avoid letting the public know of the engagement while the bridegroom was still heavily engaged in Leicestershire with another "interest."

Samala, however, was fully preoccupied with the gowns that kept arriving from London, and on two occasions the Marchioness had come to the Priory to help her inspect them and choose others with Madame Bertin.

She had assured Samala in glowing terms how thrilled the Duke was that she had accepted his proposal and how much he was looking forward to their wedding on June 2.

Now there was a strange silence before Maureen Henley said:

"This is certainly a surprise, and of course, dearest, I wish you every possible happiness."

"There is only one thing which is making me very worried and unhappy," Samala said.

"And what is—that?"

Samala felt that Mrs. Henley was diffident about asking the question.

"It is Papa. I feel he will be so lonely, and quite frankly, he will never be able to cope with the house without me."

When Mrs. Henley did not speak, Samala said:

"Of course he will have to try, and because he is already feeling a little low and depressed, I wonder if you will come over and stay for a few days while I am busy with the clothes that keep arriving, and help me try to adjust him to the fact that when I am gone he will have to manage alone."

Maureen Henley drew in her breath.

"You know I will do anything to help you, Samala," she said, "but perhaps your father will not—want me."

"Of course he will want you," Samala replied, "and there are so many things you could help me with, if you could spare the time."

Mrs. Henley folded away her embroidery.

"I am going to come back with you now," she said. "It will not take my maids long to pack, and a groom can return to the Priory with your horse, while we travel in the carriage and you can tell me everything you want me to do."

"That is kind of you," Samala said, "and I know it will cheer up Papa."

She paused, then added:

"I am afraid you will not be very comfortable, and quite frankly, if you do not like pigeon there is not going to be very much to eat."

Maureen Henley laughed and it made her look very young and attractive.

"As it happens, I hate pigeon!" she said. "Do you think your father would be offended if I brought a chicken or two with me?"

"If you put them in the kitchen the minute you arrive," Samala replied, "he will never know it is not one of ours, which we are far too careful to kill at the moment because otherwise we would have no eggs."

Mrs. Henley laughed again. Then, almost like two School-girls, they were both laughing.

When the carriage left an hour later there was quite a pile of food on board, and also a case of claret.

With a twinkle in her grey eyes Maureen Henley said:

"I think I must tell you, Samala, that as I have been a little run-down lately, the Doctor has ordered me a special claret as a tonic. Since I must bring it with me, I should feel very embarrassed if you and your father did not join me."

Samala gave a little cry of delight, then bent forward and kissed her on the cheek.

"You understand," she said, "but do be very, very careful. You know how proud Papa is."

The smile vanished from Maureen Henley's lips.

"Yes—I know," she said in a strange voice, and turned away her head as she spoke.

They drove back to the Priory along the twisting, narrow lanes, talking together like two girls of the same age.

Only when they reached the Priory, which looked very beautiful in the last glory of the afternoon sun, did Samala feel a little worried in case her plans went awry.

"I am afraid your footman will have to carry up your luggage," she said. "Poor old Brigstock is crippled with rheumatism and is incapable of carrying anything."

"James will bring up my luggage and also take the other things we have brought into the kitchen," Maureen said in a low voice.

Samala smiled at her and, getting out of the carriage first, ran up the steps and across the Hall to the Study.

As she expected, her father was alone and Mr. Owen had left.

"I have good news, Papa," she said. "There is so much for me to do before I marry that I have asked Maureen Henley to come here and help me, and she has very kindly agreed."

"I wondered where you had gone," the Earl replied, "but how can Mrs. Henley possibly stay here?"

"Why not? We have plenty of room."

Her father did not smile, and she added:

"She will not mind."

"I mind," he said sharply, "but—"

Whatever else he had been about to say died on his lips, for at that moment Maureen Henley appeared in the doorway.

She was looking very attractive. At the same time, astonishingly, her eyes were worried and her voice when she spoke seemed almost to tremble.

"If you do not—want me," she said to the Earl, "I will of course keep the—carriage and—go home."

"Of course I want you," the Earl replied, and added hastily: "At least, Samala does, and I am very grateful for you coming to help her when she has no mother."

He walked across the room as he spoke and took Maureen Henley's hand in his.

"It is only," he added, and his voice sounded very deep, "that I could not bear you to be uncomfortable."

"I shall be very comfortable," she replied, "because I will be with Samala, and—you. I cannot tell you how much I have missed you—both."

As she spoke it seemed that she had forgotten to take her hand from the Earl's.

Then abruptly, so abruptly that it was almost rude, the Earl walked back to his desk, as if he felt protected by it, and said in a very different tone of voice:

"You will not be here for long, since Samala is being married, as I expect she has already told you, on the second of June."

The next two days were very difficult, Samala thought afterwards.

They would be laughing at something that had amused them all, then suddenly the Earl's mood would change and he would lapse into an uncomfortable silence, or else with a muttered excuse get up from the table and leave the room, not to return.

When they were not actually eating together there was little sign of him, and Samala wondered what he

53

found to occupy himself with in the woods of the unkept garden, or riding over the unploughed fields.

She knew with an instinct that made words unnecessary that Maureen Henley loved her father, and she was almost certain that he loved her.

"What can I do about them?" she asked herself, and found herself lying awake thinking about their problems, when she wanted really to think about her own life and what lay ahead.

She could not bear to think of her father being unhappy, for until now he had filled her whole life, and she loved him more than it was possible to say to him, or to anybody else.

She knew she would be miserable if she thought of him as being lonely in the great empty house where there was only Mrs. Brigstock, who was growing blind, and old Brigstock, who was really useless to look after him.

If Maureen Henley missed the large staff of excellent servants she employed at her own house, she certainly showed no sign of it.

She sometimes required Samala to do up one of her gowns, but otherwise she looked after herself very ably without a lady's-maid.

She was also very content to sleep in the beautiful room where it was rumoured that Queen Elizabeth herself had slept, but where everything was now falling into disrepair and even the curtains on the bed were tattered and torn.

"I cannot bear it!" Maureen said one evening when, on going up to bed, she and Samala found that in her bedroom one of the legs had broken off a fine old Elizabethan chair which had collapsed from wood-rot.

"We must get it mended," she said as they picked it up from the floor.

"We cannot afford to," Samala answered. "In fact, the attics at the top of the house contain a number of chairs like this, all broken, and although Papa tried to mend some of them, they are still not safe to use."

Maureen sat down on the side of the bed in a gesture of despair.

"I cannot bear it!" she said again. "This is the most beautiful house I have ever seen in my life and is a part of history. We cannot just let it crumble into dust when it should be a heritage for the future."

"I know," Samala replied. "I feel like that, but what can Papa do? He has no money, and he is far too proud to be a fortune-hunter."

There was a little silence after she had spoken. Then, as if she felt she had said too much, Samala jumped to her feet and kissed Maureen, saying:

"There is no use in 'crying over spilt milk,' as my Nanny used to say, and 'what cannot be . . . cured must be endured.' "

"That is true of some problems," Maureen answered, "but there must be a different answer to this one."

"Then I hope you find it," Samala said lightly, "because Papa and I have tried, and failed."

She said good-night and went to her own room, knowing that she had been right in thinking that Maureen Henley loved her father and that the only difficulty lay in him.

When she heard him come upstairs, she went along in her dressing-gown to the Master-bedroom, in which the Earl slept in the bed of his ancestors, their coat-of-arms emblazoned on the faded damask over the pillows.

"I came to say good-night, Papa."

"I am glad you did," he replied. "I was thinking as I came upstairs how much I shall miss you when I am alone here, and the only sound will be the squeaks of the mice in the wainscotting."

There was a depressed note in his voice, and Samala said:

"At least the Priory is beautiful, and when you look at it you can forget its dilapidated state."

"Unfortunately, I cannot forget," the Earl replied. "I am also acutely conscious that it is like an injured person who needs attention."

"But I would rather live here than in Mrs. Henley's house," Samala persisted. "It is ugly, pompous, stiff, and I know she feels that she never really belongs, as we feel we belong here."

"It is hers," the Earl objected, "and she can afford to live in style."

"I am sure Mama would say that is very cold comfort. It is love that counts in a house, Papa, and that is what the Priory has always given us. I am sure you are conscious, as I am, of love from the Wynns who have lived here for generations and who love us because we are one of them."

Her father put his arm round her and held her close to him.

"I love your imagination and your clever little brain, my dearest," he said. "I only hope the ghosts of our ancestors which you think are all round us will enjoy what I have to say to them, because when you are gone I shall have nobody else to talk to."

"I hope they will make you laugh," Samala said. "It makes me want to cry to think that you will be lonely, and I can do nothing about it. Maureen Henley will be terribly lonely too, and I cannot help her either. Oh, dear, if I am happy I want everybody I love to be happy too!"

She put her arms round her father's neck and kissed him affectionately, then slipped away, thinking that perhaps she had given him something to consider which might prevent him from falling asleep for some time.

* * *

The next day, instead of seeming closer, Maureen Henley and her father appeared to go out of their way to avoid each other, and if they exchanged six words during the day, Samala was not aware of it.

In fact, her father was not at luncheon, and it was only when dinner came that they all sat down to what was an exceptionally good meal because it consisted of food that Maureen had ordered to be sent over from her own house.

To the Earl's surprise, there was also champagne, instead of the claret they had been drinking every night.

"What is this?" he asked when he saw the bottle standing in the ice-cooler that Samala had brought to the table.

"When I saw my Doctor," Maureen answered, "he said he thought the claret had done me a great deal of good, and I could return to a lighter drink. As I do not like still white wine and find it rather acid, on his instructions I have chosen to drink champagne, and you must tell me if you think my choice is a good one."

She spoke so ingenuously that the suspicion died in the Earl's eyes, and without saying any more he opened the bottle and filled their glasses.

When dinner was over and her father had eaten it without comment, although the dishes were delicious and contained cream and many other ingredients which they could seldom afford, Maureen Henley raised her glass.

"I think," she said, "as this is the first time we have had champagne, we should drink Samala's health. I am praying, as I know you are, My Lord, that she will be very, very happy."

"Of course," the Earl replied a little heavily.

They both raised their glasses to Samala, then she said:

"It is no use . . . I cannot do it . . . I cannot leave Papa . . . alone here with nobody to look after him!"

The Earl and Maureen stared at her as she went on:

"I thought I could go away and things would be all right . . . without me . . . but I know the Brigstocks are too old and too decrepit to do a tenth of the things I do . . . and it would be cruel and selfish of me to think only of my own . . . happiness, and leave Papa here without . . . proper food, and with the place growing more dirty and dilapidated than it is already."

She turned towards her father as she said:

"Please, Papa, will you send a groom over to tell the Marchioness that I have . . . changed my mind? I am going to stay here with you . . . and the Duke will have to find himself . . . another bride."

As she spoke she got up from the table and ran from the room.

Maureen Henley put down her glass, while the Earl just stared at the chair in which his daughter had been sitting as if he could not believe what he had heard. Then he said:

"She is just being hysterical because she is being married in such ridiculous haste. She will be all right in the morning."

"I do not believe Samala is ever hysterical," Maureen answered, "and I can understand exactly what she feels."

"I know! I know!" the Earl replied. "But there is nothing I can do about it."

There was silence, and as Maureen did not speak he said:

"How can I do anything? You can see the mess I am in."

"Samala understands that. That is why she knows she cannot leave you."

"She has to leave me," the Earl said sharply. "I was surprised she accepted him, but at the same time, Buckhurst, as you probably know, is not only a very wealthy man but a great sportsman. No-one could help admiring a man who has won the Derby twice, and I understand will undoubtedly win the Gold Cup this year."

Maureen was still silent, and after a moment he went on:

"I visited Buckhurst Park several times when I was a boy. It is magnificent, and the Estate is a model of its kind. Samala will have everything—everything!"

"How can she accept that and—worry about you?"

"You will have to talk to her."

"I do not think she will listen to me."

"Then what can I do?" he asked. "I cannot allow her to throw away her chance of living as she should do just for—my sake."

Again there was a long silence before Maureen said in a hesitating voice:

"I think Samala—when she asked me here—thought that I might be—able to help you."

Her words seemed almost to vibrate on the air despite having been spoken so softly that they were only barely audible. Then the Earl said harshly:

"You must know what I feel about you, as I have for a very long time, but I have nothing to offer you —nothing!"

Maureen Henley did not speak. Her voice seemed to have died in her throat, but she put her hand very gently palm upwards on the table.

The Earl's hand closed over it, and she felt his fingers, strong, insistent, squeezing hers until they were almost bloodless. Then he said:

"I want you—you know I want you—but I am humiliated and ashamed at having nothing to offer you."

Maureen found her voice.

"Only the most beautiful house in England, and —you!"

* * *

Upstairs in her own bedroom, Samala prayed.

She felt she had done everything she could, and the only possible help at this particular moment must come from God.

She knew her perception had been right when she

had become aware that Maureen loved her father and her father loved Maureen, not perhaps in the same way he had loved her mother, but because she was a perfect companion as well as a sweet and very lovable person.

Looking back, Samala knew now that in these last years she should have persuaded her father to play a greater part in County affairs and spend more time socially with his friends.

She should have swept away his objections and invited more people to the Priory, even if they had little to offer their guests.

"Papa is a host in himself, and the right people would not worry what they ate and drank so long as they could talk to him, and realise how clever, intelligent, and charming he is," she told herself.

Her excuse for not doing anything was that she had been so young, and also so content to be with her father alone, that she had not realised that as a man he needed a woman whom he could love and who would love him.

Also, she thought now, if God was merciful, her father might still have an heir to follow him in the long tradition of the title and the Estate passing from father to son.

"I know if he will marry Maureen everything will be all right," she told herself, and yet she was afraid that at the last moment the pride of the Wynns would prove stronger and more indomitable than love.

"Please, dear God . . . please help him," Samala prayed.

She thought how often her prayers had been answered, and yet, equally, how her desperate pleas for money had been ignored.

Then it struck her that in this case the two were synonymous.

She was sure, since her father loved Maureen and she loved him, that the fact that she had money and a lot of it was not and could not be important beside the wonder of their love.

Samala sat at the open window looking out into the night, watching the stars coming out in the sky. Then it struck her that perhaps she should pray for herself.

She was not so stupid that she did not realise that the Duke in asking her to become his wife did not love her, for the obvious reason that he had never seen her.

Because she was extremely well read, she was aware that where Royalty and great aristocrats were concerned, their marriages were always arranged.

It was not a question of two people meeting each other and falling in love, but was one of breeding, suitability, environment, and also where it was financially advantageous both to the bride and groom that the marriage should take place.

Samala was aware that this had begun with the legal Contract of Marriage according to Roman Law, which had been entirely an exchange of land, goods, or money.

The Contract had been taken for legal approval to a Priest, because in most cases he was the only person in the village who could read.

Together with the Civil Contract and the exchange of goods had come the Priest's blessing, which gradually became the Church Service of Marriage.

The Duke of Buckhurst required a wife because it was the correct thing for him to marry, Samala reasoned, and he would eventually require an heir to the title.

That he had chosen her was incomprehensible, unless, for some strange reason which she could not even begin to understand, he had preferred the Kenwyn family to all the other aristocrats who she was certain would have been only too proud and willing to have an alliance with the Duke of Buckhurst.

"I am lucky, so very, very lucky," she said to the stars. "But, please, greedy though it may seem, I want more. I want him to love me, and although it may be difficult for him to do so, please use your magic."

She drew in her breath and went on in a whisper:
"When he sees me, let his heart leap towards me so

that he will know that I am the bride that Fate has chosen for him, and we have met again after perhaps a thousand years in which we have been apart."

It was all part of her reading, her dreams, and her fantasies, and she could clearly see it all happening.

Yet, it seemed to her that the Duke would not be wearing the ordinary conventional clothes of this present day and age, but the shining silver armour of chivalry, while she would be in the long-sleeved gown of Mediaeval times with a pointed head-dress from which a long white veil flowed to the ground.

Then she laughed at her own ideas.

"I should certainly look very strange if that is how I appeared as a bride!"

But even as she laughed, she knew her heart was still reaching up to the stars and she was praying for love.

She heard the door open behind her, and for a moment it was hard to come back to earth as she felt almost as if she were floating high above it on a magic carpet.

Then she turned her head, and by the light of the candle she had lit by her bed she saw Maureen looking for her.

She jumped up from the window as Maureen crossed the room and put her arms round her, and she could feel her heart beating excitedly.

"Oh, dearest, dearest!" she exclaimed. "It is all right! Your father loves me. We are to be married, and I am to live here in this glorious, beautiful house and look after him."

Samala gave a cry of delight.

Then she realised that tears were running down Maureen's cheeks and her eyes were shining like the stars.

But she was also laughing with sheer happiness.

Chapter Four

The Duke arrived home the night before his wedding in an exceedingly bad temper.

He was honest enough to admit that some of this was his own fault, in that he had been beguiled by the Baroness into staying in Leicestershire for longer than he had intended.

Again, when he had meant to leave London earlier, he found that her husband had left for an important meeting in Holland, and she was therefore alone in the Embassy.

The temptation, or rather the temptress herself, was too alluring to resist, and the Duke continued a liaison which was all the more intense and fiery because they were both aware that time was running out and a bride was waiting for him in the country.

He still of course loathed the idea of being pressured into marriage after having fought against it for so long, and it did not make things any better to learn that Edmund was making the very most of his position as heir presumptive.

He was even declaring that he very much doubted if the Duke would father a son, alleging that soon after he was born Buck had been cursed by a Witch who had prophesied that no child of his would ever inherit the Dukedom.

This was entirely a fabrication of Edmund's devious mind, and the majority of people laughed and ignored such nonsense.

But the Duke knew that his enemies—actually he had quite a number—would make the most of the story, and it was in fact the kind of lie that he most disliked, because it could only have come from somebody of Edmund's calibre.

The Duke therefore found consolation and forgetfulness in the arms of the Baroness, whose charms seemed to be magnified simply because he was well aware that he should be at home greeting his relatives who would be arriving in force to stay at Buckhurst Park for the wedding.

When finally he started off from London, everything went well until one of his leading horses dropped a shoe.

This was not an unusual occurrence, but it always infuriated anybody concerned with making a record.

Although fortunately the Duke had spare horses lodging on all the main roads, especially that from London to Buckhurst Park, it meant that he had to proceed slowly and carefully for over five miles before he could change horses.

Naturally this increased the delay, and when finally he drove down the drive of ancient oak trees and saw his house in the distance, he was aware that he would be late for dinner, which was something he disliked more than anything else.

Because he had what his Nanny had referred to when he was small as "a black monkey on his shoulder," it did not make him feel any better to notice the huge Marquee set up a short distance from the house, where the tenants and employees would be entertained tomorrow.

He regarded it scowlingly and had an impulse to turn his horses round and go straight back to London.

Then as he thought of it he could hear the Baroness say in her soft, seductive, broken English:

"I shall be waiting for you, Buck darling, and you know I would never do anything to interfere in your life in any way, but I am alvays here, if you want me."

As she made this touching declaration her red lips had been very close to his, and the exotic Parisian perfume she used seemed as enticing as the invitation in her eyes and the pressure of her soft arms round his neck.

"The Baroness is waiting," he told himself now, "but so is the boring, gauche young woman my sisters have chosen for me as a bride."

At the moment everything that marriage meant to him seemed to sweep over him like a tidal wave, and he felt drowned in the horror of it.

He could imagine all too clearly the boredom of listening to the ill-informed chatter of a girl who had had little experience of life and even less of men.

He was used to the cut and thrust, the *double entendres*, and what he recognised to be a duel of words that inevitably ended in the contact of two excited bodies.

He was also loathing the idea of seeing the amused smiles on the lips of his relatives and friends as he came down the aisle a married man, encumbered with a wife he had not chosen for himself but who was suitable because her lineage was as old as his.

"Suitable!" the Duke exclaimed to himself, and made the word sound almost like an oath.

He thought now, too late, that he had been a fool.

If he had to marry he should have chosen a woman from his own world; there were plenty of widows who would have accepted the responsibility of being his Duchess without any difficulty.

She would also have kept him amused by arranging parties of his special friends and being sophisticated enough to close her eyes to any indiscretions on his part, while he would do the same for her.

Instead of which, not thinking it over carefully as he did with any new project, he had relied on his sisters to choose his wife.

They of course had no idea except the conventional one—that she should be young and of a good family, and therefore obviously competent to produce the sons that were so essential to the succession.

Vaguely at the back of his mind he remembered that he had added his own proviso to this—that she should be pure and innocent—and he thought he must have been demented to think of anything so foolish or so incredibly boring.

What did such ideas matter when what he wanted and what he should have insisted upon was a woman like the Baroness, but without the encumbrance of a husband?

There was a dark look on the Duke's face as he alighted from his Phaeton and walked up the wide grey stone steps, which were partially covered by a red carpet, and in through the magnificently carved stone doorway.

The Major Domo was waiting to greet him, besides the Butler and at least a dozen footmen.

"Welcome home, Your Grace!" the Major Domo said respectfully.

The Duke nodded to him, and without asking any questions walked up the exquisitely carved and gilded staircase towards his own apartments.

His feeling of horror at what lay ahead was not assuaged by finding that the passages as well as the Hall had all been decorated with white flowers.

When he reached the Master Suite and entered his own bedroom, which, redesigned and embellished when the house was rebuilt by his grandfather, was so splendid as to be awe-inspiring, he was again assailed by the fragrance of flowers, which merely increased his irritation.

This came not from his own bedroom, where he would undoubtedly have thrown them out the window, but from the *Boudoir* next door, which connected his room with that which had always been used by the Duchesses of Buckhurst.

Even to think of it increased the Duke's anger, because the bed, inherited from the time of Charles II, was a riot of golden angels, hearts, and coronets, while the ceiling, painted by an Italian Master, depicted Aphrodite embracing Ares, the God of War.

The Duke walked into his bedroom, where his valet was waiting, and said disagreeably:

"Open the windows! The stink of flowers is overpowering!"

"It's the white lilies, M'Lord," his valet replied. "Her Ladyship thought they was appropriate for the *Boudoir* and the Bridal Chamber."

The Duke's lips tightened, but by a superhuman effort of self-control he refrained from expressing his feelings on the subject.

Only as he bathed in cold water did he begin to feel some of his tension and anger ebbing away, and he remembered that it would be a mistake for anyone other than his sisters to realise his true feelings.

He was aware that in a house packed with his relatives it was going to be extremely difficult to keep them from learning first that he had never seen the girl he was to marry, and secondly that he loathed not only the whole idea of marriage but also the woman who had so complacently accepted him.

He had not until this moment thought of her as being a person, but just as a wife that he did not want.

Now he thought that she must in fact be a type of woman he loathed, that is to say a "social climber," a female who would put up with any husband, whatever he was like, so long as he could give her a title and provide her with the comforts that went with it.

Too late, it seemed to him that he had been much too arbitrary in insisting that his wedding should take place within a month.

It was obvious that no woman with any pride would accept such conditions, especially when it was made clear that he did not intend even to see her or to make the gesture of proposing to her personally.

At the back of his mind he remembered reading a letter from his sister saying that a number of the parents they had approached first had turned him down.

But because Elizabeth had been too tactful to state the real reason for this, the Duke supposed it must have been because of the speed at which the marriage had to take place.

"The whole thing is a mess from start to finish!" he said aloud.

He knew that actually there was nobody but himself to blame, although that did not make things seem any better.

At last he was ready, and his valet was aware that nobody could look more magnificent or more impressive than the Duke in full evening-dress.

His satin breeches became him, and his silk stockings showed off his fine legs, which every bootmaker had claimed were perfectly formed for a riding-boot.

Below his knee the garter glittered, just as his decorations did on his well-fitting evening-coat.

His cravat was a poem in itself, but the Duke did not even glance in the mirror as he walked from the room, thinking as he did so that this was his last night of freedom.

Because he felt he had nothing to celebrate in his marriage, he had refused all suggestions from his friends that he should have a bachelor-party.

He had attended too many in the past not to find them a bore: the guests always drank too much, the jokes were bawdy, and the bridegroom doubtless felt ill for at least forty-eight hours from over-indulgence.

The Duke had wanted to spend his last night with the Baroness, and he only wished he could have her with him now, instead of having to face the curious, speculative, and amused glances of his relatives when he greeted them downstairs.

He anticipated the worst, and when a few hours later he retired to bed, the Duke knew he had underestimated how unpleasant it all would be.

He thought the toasts that were drunk to him at dinner were all insincere, and the gushing flattery of his female relatives was false.

He thought also that of the thirty people who sat down to dinner in the huge Baronial Dining-Room, there was not one, with the exception of his sister Elizabeth, for whom he had the slightest feeling of affection.

The dinner was delicious, the wines were superb, but as far as the Duke was concerned he might have been eating sawdust and drinking ditch-water.

As he sat at the head of the long table laden with the gold candelabra and gold ornaments which had been in the family for years, all he could think of was that tomorrow night and every night after this a strange woman would be sitting at the end of his table whom he was obliged to call his wife.

He was aware that his moodiness was affecting the ladies who sat on either side of him.

After doing their utmost to make him reply to their animated remarks, they looked at him out of the corners of their eyes and talked instead to their dinner-partners on their other side.

Only when the ladies had withdrawn and the port was being passed round the table did the Marquis move to sit next to the Duke and say a little hesitantly:

"I hope we have arranged everything to your satisfaction, Buck. Elizabeth and Margaret have certainly worked hard to please you."

"If you were pleasing me," the Duke replied, "I would not be here at this moment!"

The Marquis sighed before he replied:

"I know that, but at the same time, as you have been in London, I expect you have heard how Edmund is behaving."

"I have!"

"He is spouting forth a pack of lies," the Marquis said angrily, "to anybody who will listen to him, and unfortunately there are always a few who will do that."

The Duke's lips tightened but he did not reply, and after a moment the Marquis went on:

"At the same time, I hear he is desperately worried. The Money-Lenders are calling in their loans."

"He should have expected that," the Duke remarked.

"Of course," the Marquis agreed. "But I do not like the situation. Desperate men do desperate things, Buck, as you well know."

"I should not imagine Edmund could do anything more desperate than marry Lottie!" the Duke said.

The Marquis sighed again.

"I hope you are right, but I just feel uncomfortable about the whole situation."

"What do you think I feel?" the Duke asked savagely.

The Marquis did not reply, and somebody else engaged the Duke's attention.

Fortunately, the evening ended early, as the majority of the relatives were getting on in age, and many of them had long distances to travel after the wedding was over.

The Marchioness had made it quite clear to them that they could not continue to stay at Buckhurst Park, since the Duke would be there for the first few nights of his honeymoon.

Elizabeth was in fact guessing, because she had no idea what her brother's plans would be after he had married.

She had written two letters to him asking him where he was going for a honeymoon, but he had not replied, and she had merely hoped that he had made his arrangements with Mr. Dalton and left it at that.

She was quite sure that the first night at any rate would be spent at Buckhurst Park, and she had therefore made it quite clear that the wedded couple were to be left alone.

She had also hoped to have a talk with Buck early in the day before the party arrived, but as he was so late, she thought despairingly that there was nothing more she could do to ensure that everything went off well.

She could only pray that the expression that had been on his face all through dinner would not frighten Samala from the moment they were married.

Every visit she made to the Priory had made her grow fonder of her future sister-in-law, besides making her more convinced than she was already that she was everything that Buck had asked for in a wife.

At the same time, her friends in London could not prevent themselves from telling her how alluring the Baroness was, and how she and Buck had spent every moment of their time together since they had arrived from Leicestershire.

"Why did that woman have to come into Buck's life at this particular moment?" Elizabeth asked her husband.

"She is very attractive!"

"All Buck's women have been that, but she sounds rather worse than the rest."

"If you mean she is a Siren," the Marquis said slowly, "then I suppose that is the type Buck has always favoured. I could name half-a-dozen of his beauties who had a serpent-like grace about them, and in consequence were regarded as dangerous by women like yourself."

"Of course I think they are dangerous," Elizabeth replied, "but I love Buck, and you know, Arthur, how fond you are of him, and we want him to be happy in his marriage. But what chance will a child like Samala have if she has to compete with a woman like the Baroness?"

Because he had no answer to this, the Marquis had merely shrugged his shoulders, and Elizabeth thought despairingly that there was nothing she could do that she had not already done.

The following morning was brilliant with sunshine, and at least it was some satisfaction to know that the garden, where the gardeners had been working feverishly ever since the wedding had been announced, was a bower of beauty.

So was the Church, and as the guests filled it with a kaleidoscope of colour, the Marchioness thought that Samala would appreciate the wreaths of white flowers that had been arranged round the Chancel and the star-like white orchids that covered the altar.

'They are like her,' she thought, and was surprised that she should be so poetical.

Samala was already being entranced by the decorations in the village which they passed through before they reached the Church which was just inside the great Park.

Because the villagers were thrilled that the Duke should be married, which meant a party for them and the promise of fireworks in the evening, they had decorated their cottages as well as making two triumphal arches through which the bride must pass before she reached the Church.

Because both the Earl and Samala lived in a world of their own, struggling with their own problems, they had no idea of how much they were admired locally and how affectionately people felt about them.

The Earl would have been particularly surprised if he had realised that because he was so handsome and people thought him brave under the difficulties of his position, he was pitied and at the same time respected.

"'E be a real gent'man, tha's wot 'e be," the local farmers and their wives said, "an' it's a cryin' shame 'e 'asn't got two h'pennies to rub together. An' if 'e 'ad, 'e'd be sharin' it wi' someone, and that's the truth!"

Because they were sorry for him, they went out of their way to do small things for the Kenwyn Estate and to obviate extra expense from damage and flood which might otherwise have cost the Earl money that he could not afford.

Because Samala was like her mother, they loved her too.

The Countess had had nothing to give them except kindness, love, and understanding.

Although their cottages leaked and they knew it was no use asking for repairs, the fact that she was there and would call on them if they were ill and listen to their troubles meant more than rain-resistant roofs and newly painted doors, which could be found just over the border on the Duke's Estate.

Then, after all these years of hoping he would marry, that the Duke should have chosen as his wife somebody they knew and were fond of was deeply appreciated, besides delighting everybody who lived on both Estates.

The Duke would have been astonished if he had realised how the choice had enhanced his own reputation.

"He's got an eye for the right horse, and now I knows h's one for the right wife," one Tradesman said to another, and their wives told each other that there'd never be a prettier bride than Her Ladyship, whatever her wedding-gown might be like.

Because nothing could be hidden from local eyes and ears, it was soon learnt that Samala's wedding-gown, like her trousseau, was a present from the Marchioness.

It came from London, and speculation about it

73

excited all the young girls of her age, as well as their mothers, their grandmothers, and their great-grandmothers.

When Samala and her father entered the village in the Duke's largest and most impressive carriage, drawn by four superb horses, the road was lined with women waving their handkerchiefs.

They watched the carriage pass, then ran as quickly as they could through a secondary entrance into the Park.

The carriage went on to pass through the main gate with the rampant griffon carried on the stone gate-posts, and the wrought-iron gates themselves surmounted by the Ducal coronet.

By the time the horses drew up outside the small grey stone Church, the crowd outside seemed enormous.

Then as Samala was helped out of the carriage there was a loud gasp of excitement at the sight of her gown.

The Marchioness had chosen it with care, and it was as beautiful as any bride could wish for in her dreams.

The bodice of soft white gauze with a very full skirt accentuated the tininess of Samala's waist, and the veil which covered her face made her appear ethereal and almost like a nymph or a sprite which had risen from a lake.

On her head she wore a tiara belonging to the Buckhurst collection. It was not the overwhelming, crown-like one which the Duchesses had always worn for the Opening of Parliament and other State occasions, but had the form of a tiny wreath of flowers.

With the tiara on her fair hair catching the sunlight, she seemed to carry it with her from the brightness outside into the darkness of the Nave.

Holding on to her father's arm, Samala felt as if she were moving in a dream and what was happening could not be true.

It was one thing to think she was to be married, but

now the moment had come when she had left home and was walking up the aisle towards the man who was to be her husband.

She felt as if she were telling herself one of her usual fanciful stories, but it had become real and was no longer just a part of her imagination.

And yet the soft music of the organ, and the rustle of the congregation as she passed them, was like the music of the wind in the trees, and all the time she was conscious of her feet carrying her nearer and nearer to the Duke.

The walk up the aisle seemed to take a long time, but suddenly she was beside him, and she glanced up at him from under her veil and he seemed to fill the whole Church, until there was nothing and nobody but him.

* * *

It was extremely hot in the Ball-Room, and the queue to shake hands with the Duke and Samala seemed endless.

Their names were announced, but to Samala they were unknown and completely meaningless, and the Butler's stentorian voice seemed to blend with the endless stream of congratulations until it became like the continuous roar of waves on the sea-shore.

"Many congratulations, Buck, and I do hope you will be happy!"

"It is lovely to meet you, and we do hope we shall see a lot of you and your husband!"

"My very good wishes for your happiness!"

"My husband and I hope to entertain you as soon as you come back from your honeymoon!"

"Every possible good wish to you both!"

On and on, and Samala found her voice saying automatically over and over again, "Thank you," "thank you," and tried to focus her eyes on each person, but found it somehow impossible.

Then at last, when she felt breathless with the heat and they had been standing for nearly two hours in the same position, she was aware that the Duke was moving away from her and wondered if she was meant to follow him.

Then the Marquis was beside her to put a glass of champagne into her hand, saying as he did so:

"You must be tired, but you have been splendid and everybody is admiring you."

"Thank you," Samala replied.

She wondered where the Duke had gone, and looked through the sea of guests, thinking that because he was so tall she must see him.

It had been impossible for them to speak to each other when they had left the Church in the open carriage, for as the horses moved off there had been deafening cheers all the way to the house, while the children and the villagers threw flowers into the open carriage, little bunches of roses and daisies, "pinks" from the cottage gardens, bouquets of honeysuckle, and dog-roses from the hedgerows.

It was all so touching, Samala thought, and she tried to thank those who were cheering her by smiling and waving, and she thought the Duke was doing the same on his side of the carriage.

Inside the guest house there were half-a-dozen servants waiting to escort them along the passage which led to the Ball-Room, and Samala had only a quick impression of white flowers, paintings and flags, and high, painted ceilings, before there was the noise of voices.

As they entered the Ball-Room the Marchioness showed them where they were to stand by the door against a background of huge vases filled with white Madonna lilies.

"You look lovely, dearest," she said to Samala. "All the young women were crying because your gown is so beautiful, knowing they would never be able to have a lovelier one at their own wedding."

Samala gave a little laugh and glanced at the Duke

to see if he was laughing too, but his head was turned away from her as he talked to the Marquis on his other side.

Then the guests began to arrive, and there was no chance to do anything but respond politely to their good wishes, and now as she searched in the crowd for the Duke, her father put his arm round her and Maureen kissed her.

"It was such a lovely wedding," she exclaimed, "and you looked just like a Princess in a fairy-story!"

Samala smiled with delight because that was what she wanted to hear. Then Maureen added in a low voice:

"I am praying, dearest, that you will be as happy as I am."

Yesterday, the day before her own wedding, very early in the morning, Samala had attended her father's and Maureen's wedding in the little Church where she had been christened.

Unlike her own, it had been a very quiet, private ceremony, because the Earl had thought it embarrassing that he should be marrying before his daughter, until Samala and Maureen had convinced him that it was the sensible thing to do.

"Not only do I want to be at your wedding, Papa," Samala said, "but you know that once I am gone, if you are not married, Maureen would have to go home and leave you alone, and that would worry me. So please get married as quickly as you possibly can."

Spurred both by his own feelings and theirs, the Earl had obtained a Special Licence, and the local Vicar, who was a friend, agreed to keep everything secret.

Nobody noticed the three people slipping into the village Church at nine o'clock in the morning after the men had gone into the fields to work and the women were busy in their cottages.

It had been a Service without music, and yet, Samala thought, the angels were singing because her father would be happy, and no-one could have looked more radiant than his bride.

When the Earl put the ring on Maureen's finger, Samala saw the love in her step-mother's eyes and knew that her father would be well looked after, and the misery, poverty, and privation of the last years would soon be forgotten.

"I shall be very, very tactful, dearest," Maureen had said, "and try not to make your father aware that it is my money that is paying for everything. But I want him to take his rightful place in the County, for so many people have told me how much they regretted the way he had become almost a hermit instead of leading and guiding them as they wanted him to do."

Samala gave a little cry of delight.

"That is what I wanted you to say! Papa is so clever, and his brain has been wasted on just fussing about the house falling down and not being able to farm the land."

"That is all going to be changed," Maureen promised. "At the same time, I could not bear him to think that I am pushing him into doing things he does not wish to do."

"He loves you," Samala said, "so it will be easy for you to persuade him to do everything that is important."

Maureen kissed her.

"You are very wise and very sensible," she said, "and since I know I owe all my happiness to you, I can only hope that one day you will be as happy as I am."

Samala did not answer, and there was an expression on her face which made Maureen apprehensive. When she was alone with the Earl, she said a little tentatively:

"I am worried about Samala, because she is so very young, and she knows so little of the world outside this magical, fairy-like house of yours."

"She will learn about things soon enough," the Earl remarked.

"That is what makes me anxious," Maureen answered.

Because she sensed that he too lived in a world that was very different from the one in which the Duke shone so brilliantly, she did not try to inflict on him her own misgivings over Samala's future.

Instead, she vowed to herself that the Priory would be as beautiful inside as it was on the outside, and what Samala had found there in her fantasy-world she must never lose, because it was something too precious and too perfect to be spoilt by the cruelty and evil of reality.

While Samala had felt overcome by the heat and the endless hand-shaking and repetition of good wishes, the Duke had felt an anger rising up inside him to the point where he could no longer tolerate it.

All he had ever said about his hatred of being married seemed to accelerate the throbbing in his head until it became a physical pain.

He hated his relations, he hated his friends, and he was quite certain that everything they said to him was a lot of rubbish just mouthed out because it was the conventional thing to do.

He was also acutely conscious that the woman who stood by his side was now his wife.

He had not looked at her in the Church because he had no wish to do so, and after they had signed their names in the Vestry it was not he who had lifted her veil, as was traditional, but his sister Elizabeth, and he had turned his back while she did so.

He had not looked at Samala when she had taken his arm, and as they walked down the aisle to the sound of the "Wedding March" played on the organ, he thought he could hear the sniggers of the congregation, and he told himself it was like walking to the guillotine.

He had surrendered his freedom simply to prevent Lottie from wearing a Duchess's coronet, and it was a heavy price to pay.

Because he suddenly thought he could bear it no longer, when there was a gap before the next guest was announced, he left Samala's side and walked out of the Ball-Room, intending to go upstairs to his own rooms.

He met Mr. Dalton in the Hall.

"I was just coming to find you, Your Grace."

"What is it?" the Duke asked.

"I thought you would like to know that the horse you bought at Tattersall's three days ago has arrived."

"I was not expecting him until tomorrow," the Duke exclaimed.

Mr. Dalton smiled.

"I think they were glad to get him here, Your Grace. From what I have learnt, he's busy at the moment trying to break down his stall!"

"I was told he was very wild," the Duke replied. "In fact, in consequence I was the only person to bid for him."

"I hope he's not dangerous!" Mr. Dalton said in a voice of alarm.

"I hope he is!" the Duke retorted.

He went out of the front door without saying any more and walked in the direction of the stables.

Mr. Dalton watched him go, and sighed.

He knew better than anybody else what the Duke was feeling at this moment, and he could understand how the wild horse appealed to him very much more than a quiet, well-trained animal.

At the same time, he was well aware that the Duke should not be leaving his guests or, more important, his bride.

As if he thought it was his duty, he hurried in the direction of the Ball-Room in case there was anything he could do to prevent the Duke's disappearance from being noticed.

* * *

The Duke walked to the stables, and even as he reached them he heard his new acquisition making a commotion in one of the stalls.

The horse had quite an audience, consisting of a

number of stable-boys, his Head Groom, and two or three strangers who must have found the Duke's horses more interesting than the presents that were laid out in the Billiard-Room and the large five-tiered cake which had not yet been cut.

The Head Groom hurried to the Duke as soon as he appeared.

"'E be a very fine beast, Yer Grace. But Oi thinks we're gonna 'ave a bit o' trouble wi' 'im."

"I thought that myself," the Duke said with satisfaction.

He looked into the stall where the horse was doing his best to demolish the manger.

"He should be too tired after the journey to behave like this," he said.

"'E's not come far today, Yer Grace. They 'ad such difficulty in gettin' 'im yesterday to Winchpoole, where they stayed the night."

"What he needs now is exercise," the Duke said. "Saddle him!"

"Now, Yer Grace?" the Head Groom asked, looking at the Duke's wedding finery as if he could not believe the order he had been given.

"I will only take him a short distance in the Park," the Duke said.

It took the Head Groom, two second grooms and four stable-boys to get a saddle on the horse, who was living up to his name, which was *Wild Rufus*.

Only when with difficulty they led him to the bridle block and the Duke sprang into the saddle did *Wild Rufus* realise with a sense of satisfaction that he had on his back a worthy opponent.

He instantly began to show his independence and resentment at being taken to a new stable.

The Duke enjoyed every moment of it.

For the first time for several days he felt his anger, which had been like a stone in his chest, moving away, and he was concentrating not on his own problems but on an adversary who revealed a determination as strong as his own.

It took him ten minutes to get *Wild Rufus* from the stable onto the drive, and then to take him shying over the bridge which spanned the lake.

Then, as if the horse thought he might as well enjoy himself, he started to move across the Park under the trees.

On the other side of it there was an excellent gallop, which was a piece of flat land where the Duke knew he would be able to gallop the devil out of *Wild Rufus*.

The Duke was aware that it was dangerous to go at all fast in the Park where there were rabbit-holes under the trees and the ground was rough.

He therefore held *Wild Rufus* on a tight rein, aware that without spurs and a whip he was at a slight disadvantage.

At the same time, he knew that with his brilliant expertise where horses were concerned, it was only a question of time before *Wild Rufus* acknowledged him to be his Master, and they would declare a tentative truce for today, at any rate.

Because he had broken in so many horses and because to do so gave him more satisfaction than any other sport in which he was regularly engaged, the Duke was enjoying himself.

He kept *Wild Rufus* under control by sheer force as they moved nearer and nearer to where he could give the horse his head and let him gallop until he was too exhausted to fight any longer.

Then as he passed under almost the last large oak tree in that part of the Park, from a bush at the foot of it a speckled deer rose suddenly almost at *Wild Rufus*'s feet and flashed past him.

Immediately the horse reared up, snorting with terror, and because he was a very large stallion, the Duke, as he was thrown backwards, crashed his head against the lowest branch of the oak tree.

The impact of it forced him for the moment to loosen his pressure on the reins, and *Wild Rufus* with a convulsive movement flung the Duke from his back, and as he fell lashed out with his hind legs, catching him on the chest.

At the impact the Duke felt the darkness rise up towards him, and as he hit the ground he lay still.

Chapter Five

$\mathcal{T}$he Duke came back to consciousness through a long, dark tunnel.

His brain would not function and he could not think where he was or what was happening. He knew only that everything was dark.

Then as he tried to move there was a sharp, agonising pain in his chest, and the darkness covered him again.

* * *

It may have been a century or an hour later when the Duke became aware of himself and that something had happened, although he could not think what it was.

He stirred, and instantly somebody was beside him and he felt a cool hand on his forehead, and thought it was comforting.

"I—am—thirsty—"

He was not certain if he said the words or thought them, but there was a movement beside him, an arm was slipped behind his head, and there was a glass at his lips.

He drank, realising that his mouth was very dry, and what he was drinking was cool, soothing, and sweet.

He felt it slip down his throat. Then a low voice said softly:

"Go to sleep. Everything is all right. You will feel better in the morning."

He wanted to ask what had happened, but he was too tired. Again he felt the cool hand on his forehead, stroking it mesmerisingly until, as if hypnotised by the movement, he fell asleep.

* * *

The Duke awoke to find as he opened his eyes that the sun was too bright, and almost as if he had said so, somebody in the room lowered the blind.

Then he was aware that there was a man standing beside him, and as he reached forward to take hold of his wrist, the Duke knew he must be a Doctor.

"What—has—happened?" he asked, and thought to himself that his voice sounded weak and raw.

"You've had an accident, Your Grace," the Doctor replied, "but there's nothing seriously wrong with you, except concussion and a very bad bruise where your horse kicked you."

As he spoke, the Duke remembered what had happened and how *Wild Rufus* had reared up.

"I hit—my—head," he said almost as if he spoke to himself.

"You not only hit it, you also fell on it," the Doctor said, "and as the horse kicked you, your chest will be painful. But I know Your Grace'll be glad to know that there are no bones broken, and all you have to do is to rest until you're better."

The Duke wanted to argue that the last thing he wanted to do was to stay in bed, but it was too much effort.

He closed his eyes and was aware that the Doctor was giving instructions, but he did not listen to what was being said.

* * *

There was only one candle burning by the bedside, and he thought he was alone, until he saw`there was somebody asleep in the corner of the room on a sofa which matched the hanging on the bed.

For a moment he thought he must be imagining things, for it was so improbable that anybody would be sleeping in his bedroom.

Then in the light from the candles he could see that a head which had very pale, fair hair rested against the satin cushions.

He was puzzling over it when, as if the fact that he was awake communicated itself to the person on the sofa, she stirred, sat up, and looked across the room at him.

He gave an exclamation as a young woman rose and came towards him.

When he could see her clearly he thought for one moment that she was only a child. Then he saw two enquiring blue eyes looking into his, and as she smiled there was a dimple on either side of her mouth.

"You are awake!" she said. "Shall I give you a drink?"

"Who—are—you?" the Duke asked, trying to understand what was happening.

Again there was that dimpled smile before Samala said quietly:

"I expect you are finding it difficult to remember, but I do happen to be your wife!"

Now the Duke thought he really must be dreaming. Then, as if the darkness was moving away from his mind, everything that had happened came back to him.

The wedding, his anger, the heat of the Reception, the moment when he could stand it no longer and had left, to go to the stables to ride *Wild Rufus*.

As his memory stopped there, he asked:

"The horse—he is—all right?"

"Perfectly!" Samala answered. "Except that everybody is afraid of him, and he knows it! I have told him that he will have to behave better when you ride him again."

As she spoke she lifted the Duke's hand and raised the glass to his lips. Again he was drinking something smooth and sweet which slipped down his throat and took away the dryness.

"When will I be—up—again?" he asked as she took the glass from his lips.

"The Doctor has been very gloomy about it," Samala answered, "but I think that because you are so strong you will be better far sooner than he expects. Doctors are always over-cautious like fussy Nannies."

The way she spoke made the Duke want to laugh, but he knew it would hurt his chest if he did so; and instead he lay back against the pillows, which she had patted into position for him, and said:

"I feel we should be introduced to each other, and I should ask why you are nursing me. Surely it would have been easier to get a Nurse?"

"On the contrary," Samala replied. "Nurses, as you must be aware, are almost unobtainable in the country. The village Midwife, who would be only too willing to oblige, is old and keeps herself awake only with tots of gin!"

Her eyes were twinkling as she spoke, and the Duke found himself watching for her dimples.

"Then I must thank you for saving me from her ministrations!" he said. "At the same time, I feel it is a shocking imposition."

"Your valet looks after you most of the time during the day," Samala said. "In fact, I nursed my father when he broke his collar-bone out riding, and another time when he fell off a high ladder and got concussion."

"I feel sure this is not the way you envisaged starting your married life," the Duke remarked.

"I am happy to be here with you," Samala said. "While you were lying here unconscious, you looked exactly like your ancestor on the tomb in the Church."

The Duke thought for a moment. Then he said:

"I think you must mean Sir Harold Buckhurst, who went to the Crusades."

"Of course," she replied. "And that is exactly how I thought you looked the first time I saw you."

The Duke was silent for a moment. Then he asked:

"Are you saying that we have met before?"

Samala shook her head.

"No, we have never met, but I saw you and I thought . . ."

She stopped.

"I must let you rest. I will tell you all about it another time. The Doctor was most insistent that you should not be over-tired."

"I am sick of sleeping," the Duke complained petulantly, "and I am interested in what you are saying to me. If you do not finish that sentence, I shall lie awake wondering about it, and that will be very bad for me."

Samala gave a little laugh and he thought it was like the sound of a song-bird.

"Now you are blackmailing me," she said, "but if you promise to go to sleep, I will tell you that the first time I saw you was eight years ago, riding in a Steeple-Chase."

She saw a flicker of recognition in the Duke's eyes, and went on:

"You were on a magnificent black stallion and leading the field, and as I watched you I thought you looked exactly like a Crusader Knight! When I have thought about you since, I have always felt that actually you were wearing shining silver armour, and there was a cross on your shield."

She spoke with a rapt note in her voice that the Duke did not miss, and her eyes seemed to catch the light from the candles.

He knew, although it seemed very strange, that what she had seen had meant a great deal to her.

Then in a very different voice she said:

"Now you have to be good and do as you promised and go to sleep. Otherwise the Doctor will be very angry with me for tiring you and will insist on the village Midwife, with her gin bottle, coming to take my place."

The Duke could not prevent a little laugh from coming to his lips. Then, feeling the expected pain in his chest, he controlled it.

He suddenly realised he was very tired. At the same time, Samala had given him something to think about.

"Good-night," he said as he closed his eyes, and felt her hand on his forehead.

* * *

The Duke sat up in bed feeling extremely irritable.

The back of his head, which had hit the bough of the tree, ached, and the bruise on his chest made it extremely painful to move.

The Doctor had come early in the morning and prescribed nothing except rest and categorically refused to allow him to get up at least for another week.

Now, after he had been washed and shaved and the sheets and pillow-cases on his bed had been changed, he felt it was humiliating to be kept in bed as if he were a child, and the sooner he asserted himself and got dressed, the better.

"I will get up tomorrow," he said aloud to his valet.

"We'll see what Her Grace says about that," Yates replied.

The Duke stared at him in utter astonishment.

He could hardly believe that Yates, of all people, would consider anybody's orders except his own to be of any consequence.

"I will do what I want to do," the Duke snapped. "Bring me the newspapers!"

"The Doctor said, Your Grace, that you're not to use your eyes because they might have been affected by the blow on your head. Her Grace'll be along shortly, and she told me that as soon as you were ready to listen she'd read you anything you wished in the newspapers."

As if Yates knew that his Master was going to argue, he said no more and slipped out of the bedroom, closing the door behind him.

The Duke was astounded and would have thrown himself petulantly back against the pillows, if he had not realised that it would hurt him to do so.

He was just wondering whether he should ring and order Yates to return to him for further instructions when the door opened and Samala came into the room.

The Duke·had not seen her since the previous evening, and he thought as she came across to the bed that she was in fact the child he had thought her to be at first sight.

She was so slight, so thin, that it took him a moment or two to realise that her gown, which was very elegant, revealed the soft curves of her breasts.

Yet her face was that of a child, or rather, he thought to his surprise, of a very young angel! With the sunlight behind her, her hair seemed almost like a golden halo for her bright blue eyes and translucent pink-and-white skin.

For the moment she was concentrating on what she was holding in her hands, which was a bowl of small orchids of a very rare and unusual kind, which were white but changed to pink at the end of each petal.

Then as she neared the bed she looked up and smiled at him, and he saw once again the dimples that he had noticed before.

"Look what I have brought you," she said, and there was a lilt in her voice. "Your Head Gardener says you have been waiting for two years for these to flower, and what could be more appropriate than that they should do so now and cheer you up?"

The Duke looked at the vase she held out to him and said:

"They are certainly as lovely as I thought they would be."

"Where did you find them?"

"In Darjeeling, when I visited India."

Samala gave a little cry.

"You have been to India? Tell me about it. It is a country I have always longed to visit! I have read books and books about it, but nothing could be the same as actually going there."

The Duke was surprised, because although he had travelled quite extensively in his life, he had found that most women were not interested in his adventures unless they concerned themselves.

He watched Samala put the orchids down on the table by his bed, then she said in a different tone:

"Forgive me, I should have asked you first how you feel today."

The Duke frowned.

"I will not have Yates tittle-tattling to you," he said sharply. "I shall get up when I want to, and that will doubtless be tomorrow."

He expected Samala to look abashed or at least to feel rebuked by what he said, but instead she put out her hand and laid it on his.

"Please, please, be sensible," she said. "There are so many things I want you to show me, and if you take a long time getting well because you got up from bed too quickly, we shall both find it very frustrating."

The Duke looked at her in surprise.

Then as he saw the pleading in her eyes, he realised that she was completely sincere, and it flashed through his mind that she was not aware that his intention had been to leave as quickly as possible after their wedding and return to London.

Then he told himself that as that now was obviously impossible and the Baroness would have to wait, he might as well make the best of being at home, even with a wife he did not want.

Then, as if she knew what he was thinking, she said in a low voice:

"I am really not trying to stop you from doing

anything, as I know I could not do that. It is just that everybody has been so worried about you, and I have been praying very . . . very hard that you will soon be strong again."

"Does it matter so much?" the Duke asked.

"Of course it does!"

She gave a little sigh and looked round the room.

"I had no idea when I thought about you that everything that surrounds you would be so exactly right for you."

"What do you mean by that?" the Duke asked curiously.

"This house, the things in it, your horses, the people who not only serve you but love you, all make a frame which is exactly what it should be for the Knight I saw winning the Steeple-Chase."

"Do you really mean to tell me that you have thought of me ever since then?" the Duke enquired.

He asked the question mockingly, then was surprised when she looked away from him and he saw the colour creeping into her cheeks almost like the first fingers of the dawn.

It was such a long time since he had seen a woman blush that he watched her in silence until she turned her face to him and said:

"Perhaps I should not have . . . told you . . . but you must have wondered why I agreed to . . . marry you when, as far as you were concerned we had never . . . met."

The Duke looked at her in astonishment. Then he asked:

"Are you telling me that you agreed to become my wife simply because you had seen me ride in a Steeple-Chase and had thought of me ever afterwards?"

"Of course that was the reason!" Samala said. "When your sister came to see Papa with the proposition that I should marry her brother, I did not realise at first of whom she was speaking. In fact, I thought it most insulting that we were not to . . . meet before . . . our wedding-day."

She paused, then the Duke said:

"Then what did you think?"

"When she said her brother was the Duke of Buckhurst, I thought it was Fate that you should want to marry me, when I had thought of you not only in my dreams but in the thousand stories I have told myself ever since I watched you ride over that last fence, and knew that you could win . . . anything on which you set your . . . heart."

The Duke thought the way she spoke was so mesmeric that he felt as if he were being carried away into a fairy-story himself.

He remembered that race well, and because the going was hard and the fences very high and he was riding a young horse, he had thought his chances of winning were slight.

He had actually lifted his horse almost by will-power over the last fence, then down the straight to the winning-post.

When he had received the cheers and congratulations of those who had watched him, he had known he deserved them, and it seemed extraordinary now that Samala should have been watching him and understanding what a victory it had been.

"I can see you are fond of riding," he remarked.

Her eyes lit up.

"I love it more than anything else, and that is why I want to ride with you. But you must not attempt to break in *Wild Rufus* until you are really strong enough."

"Are you once again telling me what I should or should not do?" the Duke asked in an amused voice.

"Not really," Samala replied in a serious little voice. "I am telling you that you are a very precious person and must not take any unnecessary risks with yourself."

The Duke thought he had received many compliments in his life, but this was perhaps the most ingenuous of them all.

"Thank you," he said. "At the same time, if you expect to keep me wrapped up in cotton-wool, you are going to find me very disagreeable and irritable about it, and it would be wise to keep out of my way."

"You have forgotten that as your wife I am here to amuse you," Samala replied, "and I have therefore planned all sorts of different ways in which we can pass the time, starting of course with the newspapers. Do you wish to hear what they said about our wedding?"

"No, I do not!" the Duke replied emphatically and without thinking.

As he spoke, he remembered how much he had hated the wedding and everything about it, and almost as if they forced themselves upon him he could see Edmund with his vulgar wife, Lottie, reading the reports in the newspapers.

Then he heard a very small voice that seemed to come from a long distance say:

"I am . . . sorry. I did not . . . mean to . . . upset you, but I had . . . no idea that you . . . hated our wedding as much as . . . all that."

Too late the Duke realised that he had spoken without consideration in front of Samala, which was exceedingly rude to say the least of it.

With an effort he forced the frown from between his eyes and said a little lamely:

"I was just wondering how many of the people who came to imbibe our champagne, drink our health, and give us their good wishes were really sincere about it, or just curious to see you."

"I think most of them were sincere, because they admire you so much," Samala answered. "You are a very distinguished man, and what is more important, you are an inspiration to sportsmen all over the country. They want to be like you, they want to win without cheating, and to follow your example, not only on the race-course but in every other way as well."

The Duke looked at her in surprise.

He could hardly believe that she was not flattering him for some personal reason of her own, and yet he felt sure that the sincerity in her voice could not be assumed.

The Duke was a very good judge of men, and those who had served with him in the Army were aware that he was a born leader.

The men he led not only admired but respected him, and they knew too that they could never put anything over on him.

He would know when a man was going to lie to save himself from punishment before he opened his lips.

While the Duke had seldom exercised that particular intuition where it concerned a woman, he knew now that Samala spoke with a sincerity that surprised him but at the same time was utterly and completely genuine.

Because he knew he had made a mistake in the way he had spoken of their wedding, he said:

"I wish I could believe that what you said is true, but there is no doubt that the English at heart are all sportingly inclined, which is something our politicians often forget when they are dealing with them."

"That is what I was thinking," Samala said, "and there is so much for you to do in the House of Lords."

The Duke raised his eye-brows, and she went on:

"I liked the speech you made about the cruelty of gin-traps and even more when you spoke against bull-baiting, which is a horrible, degrading sport which no-one should watch."

"You read my speeches?" the Duke asked in astonishment.

"Of course I do!" Samala said. "I have cut out and kept the report of every speech you have ever made."

The Duke looked at her as if he could hardly believe what he had heard, and Samala continued:

"Papa and I used to discuss them, and sometimes I longed to write to you and ask you to speak on other subjects which we thought needed to be brought to the attention not only of Their Lordships but of the public."

"Now you will be able to *tell* me what you want," the Duke said, and thought this was certainly something he had not expected from his wife.

Samala then read to him the leading articles in *The Times* and in *The Morning Post* and the Parliamentary Reports in both papers.

At first the Duke listened because he was interested in what she was reading, then he found himself thinking of how soft and musical her voice was.

He had always disliked women with hard, strident voices, but most of all he loathed those who were affected.

He remembered one beautiful woman who had beguiled him for only a very short time because he had always known when she was pretending something which she did not feel, or being gushingly effusive in a manner which sounded so contrived that it set his teeth on edge.

Then the music of Samala's voice made him close his eyes, and before he was aware of it he had fallen asleep.

* * *

Later that afternoon, when the Duke felt rested and somewhat resentful that he had spent so many hours sleeping, Samala produced various games she had found downstairs which she thought might amuse him.

"Your Curator is such a charming man," she said, "and he told me you are a good Chess-player. I am afraid you will beat me easily, but I will try to give you a game, if it would amuse you."

They played several games, in which the Duke found himself the winner but only with some difficulty.

"You are too good for me!" Samala said with a little sigh when the Duke had called "Checkmate!" with a note of triumph in his voice. "But of course, as I have already told you, you will always be the winner, whoever your opponent may be."

"You will make me very conceited if you talk like that," the Duke said.

She shook her head.

"I do not think so."

"Why do you say that?"

"Because people are conceited only when they cannot understand their own potential. You know that what you set out to achieve is yours if you approach it the right way, and that is not really conceit, but an inner knowledge that comes from those who have a power to win."

The Duke listened to her in astonishment, then he said:

"I have never heard it explained quite like that before, but I think I understand what you are trying to say."

"Papa and I used to say how sad it is that there are so few men in the world today to direct people's thoughts and minds, as the Greeks did, to what will support and develop civilisation rather than destroy it."

The way she spoke the last words made the Duke say:

"I suppose you are thinking that Napoleon had the wrong type of power."

"Exactly . . . like the Devil!" Samala replied. "Look at the suffering he caused and the misery, which will take a century to put right."

"Yet, I suppose he will always be remembered as one of the great men of history."

"It depends what you mean by 'great,'" Samala replied. "Perhaps we are conscious of him only because he is so close to us, when we should be thinking of Christ, Buddha, Marco Polo, and Christopher Columbus."

The Duke was amused and rather intrigued by this

conversation. It was certainly not the kind he had ever expected to have with a woman, and certainly not anybody who looked so young and child-like as Samala.

But already he was becoming aware that her looks were deceptive, and he had to admit that she was very lovely and unusual, and not in the least what he had expected to find in the wife he had been forced to marry.

When his dinner was brought upstairs Samala left him, and only when she returned, having been waited on by a Butler and two footmen, did she say:

"I wondered if tomorrow we could have our meals together, unless you prefer to eat alone."

"Actually I dislike it," the Duke replied, "and if it would not bore you to eat in my bedroom, then we will certainly have luncheon and dinner together here."

"I would love to," Samala replied, "and I will put on one of my most beautiful new gowns so that you will feel you are dining in state and not as an invalid."

"What you are wearing now is certainly very pretty," the Duke said, realising that perhaps he had been rather remiss in not noticing what she was wearing until now.

It was a gown of white silk and it made her look very young and even more like the small angel he had imagined her to be.

His experienced eye told him that it had been made by an expensive dressmaker, and the full skirt and tiny waist were very becoming.

"I must tell your sister that you admire my gowns," Samala said. "They were her wedding-present to me."

She thought the Duke raised his eye-brows, and she added quickly:

"I know it sounds very unconventional that Papa did not buy my trousseau, but if he had, I should have been able to have only one gown, and we would have gone hungry for at least a fortnight to pay for it!"

She gave a little chuckle of laughter, which the Duke found rather endearing, as she added:

"If I had come in my old clothes I really would have looked like the Beggar Maid marrying King Cophetua, and although it would have been very dramatic, I think perhaps you would have been rather embarrassed."

"It would certainly have given everybody something to talk about," the Duke replied.

"I am sure they were talking quite enough as it was."

There was a little silence. Then she asked:

"What made you want to marry me when every distinguished family in the country . . . would have welcomed you as a . . . son-in-law?"

The Duke drew in his breath, thinking this was a question he should have anticipated and been ready to answer. Then, because he felt it was important to Samala, he replied after only a few seconds' pause:

"I had always heard of how much your father and mother were admired in this part of the world, and what could be more sensible, when our lands border on each other's, than that our relationship should be closer?"

He saw Samala's eyes light up as if they were stars and knew he had said the right thing.

"I wondered if that might be the reason," she said, "and I am so very glad that you thought of me."

She spoke very simply, but again with a sincerity which the Duke could not misunderstand. Then she said:

"Yates is coming to get you ready to sleep, and I thought perhaps, since you are so much better, you would not want me to sleep in here tonight."

She saw the Duke hesitate and added quickly:

"In case you feel thirsty or restless in the night, I thought I might sleep in my own room but leave the doors open. Then if you call, or better still ring the little gold bell that Yates has found, I am a very light sleeper and I will come to you at once."

"I think that would be very sensible," the Duke agreed, "but, Samala, I will not disturb you because, as you say, I am very much better and quite able to look after myself."

"But you promise that if you want me you will ring the bell?"

"I promise," the Duke agreed.

She put out her hand impulsively and laid it on his.

"Thank you for all the exciting things we have done together today," she said. "It has been very wonderful for me."

There was a little pause. Then he saw the dimples on either side of her mouth as she added:

"But I am sure you would much rather have been battling with *Wild Rufus*."

Before the Duke could think of an answer, she had slipped away into the Sitting-Room next door, and Yates came in through the door from the passage.

When Yates had gone, the Duke lay thinking of Samala and how different she was from what he had expected and utterly different from anyone he had ever met before.

He told himself it was because he was profoundly ignorant on the subject of young women. Even so, he was quite sure that Samala was unusual.

He thought it very clever of his sisters to have found somebody who would assuredly play the part of the Duchess of Buckhurst with charm, and to his surprise he now felt certain that she would not bore him to distraction as he had anticipated.

For the first time he wondered what people must have thought when it was learnt that he had left his Wedding Reception to go riding on a horse that had thrown him ignominiously, resulting in his being carried back to his own house unconscious.

Knowing that he had left the Reception before any of the guests had departed, he was aware how many witnesses there must have been to exclaim at his extraordinary behavior.

In retrospect, he felt ashamed that his feelings had

been so beyond his control that he had done anything so outrageous.

He was well aware that most people would say that it was just like Buckhurst to enliven his own wedding, and his personal friends would add that they were quite certain he would never conform to convention and he had therefore felt obliged to assert himself.

However, he thought that his behaviour, whether expected or unexpected, would undoubtedly react on Samala, and he was quite certain that one person who would read the reports of the wedding with satisfaction and delight would be the Baroness.

She had been far too experienced to bewail the fact that he was getting married or even to refer to it except indirectly.

All she contrived to do was to bind him to her with bonds of passion so as to make certain that he would not only miss her when they were apart but would return to her as speedily as possible.

A speedy return could not happen now, and the Duke wondered whether his accident would make her feel that she had scored off his wife, or if she was merely frustrated that it would be so long before they could see each other again.

Then he told himself that perhaps it would be a mistake to look forward to something which had been so enjoyable continuing indefinitely.

The Duke was cynically aware what a short life his *affaires de coeur* always had, and how quickly the fires of passion could die down and become ashes.

His affair with the Baroness had begun, contrary to his intention, because she had pursued him, but at the time he had certainly regretted leaving her for a wedding which he shrank from with a loathing that was partly engendered by his hatred of his cousin Edmund.

He had been quite certain as he journeyed from London that the Baroness attracted him as no other woman had ever been able to do. But now he found himself questioning if this was true.

He thought he had in fact lost control of himself with her, just as he had when he had caused a scandal by leaving his Wedding Reception in such an abrupt manner.

He was sure that his sisters had been deeply shocked, and that a number of the guests must have expressed their condemnation of his behaviour in no uncertain terms.

Ordinarily this would not have troubled him in the slightest, but now he thought that if Samala should be aware of it, it would, as she was so young and idealistic about him, undoubtedly hurt her.

He realised that when she spoke of him as a Knight in describing what she had felt when seeing him riding in the Steeple-Chase, she was thinking of him not so much as a man but as the hero of her ideals, who filled her imagination and her dreams.

'I must be very careful not to upset her by anything I say or do,' the Duke thought before he fell asleep.

It did not strike him that this was a strange attitude for him to take up towards the wife whom he had not wanted and whom he was certain he would dislike from the first moment he saw her.

* * *

In her bedroom, Samala lay looking towards the open door which led into the flower-filled Sitting-Room and beyond that into the Duke's bedroom.

Because she had left one candle burning by his bed and he had not blown it out, she could see the golden glow in the distance, and she thought it was like the light of a star gleaming in the darkness of the night.

It was also, she thought, like a prayer that she had left with him, not only to protect him but also to help him get better and be again as she had seen him first, strong and active, riding to victory.

"He is wonderful," she told herself, "and exactly as I thought he would be!"

Then, as if she could not help it, she said a prayer of gratitude because she was so privileged to be his wife.

"Thank You, God, thank You," she whispered. "How could I have known, how could I have guessed when Papa and I were so depressed, that You had planned that this wonderful, marvellous King among men should want me as his wife?"

It was so unbelievably wonderful that she felt the tears come into her eyes.

Then she was praying again, thanking God for the fact that everything had changed overnight, and not only had she found the man of her dreams but so had Maureen.

'I know Papa will be very happy with her,' Samala thought, 'and that too is due to the Duke; for if he had not asked me to marry him, I would not have worried about Papa being left alone and would never have had the courage to bring Maureen to him and make certain he stopped being too proud to ask her to marry him.'

It was all so wonderful that Samala went on praying for a long time before she went to sleep.

* * *

She awoke with a start, feeling that something had disturbed her, and because she was not certain whether or not she had heard the Duke's bell or his voice calling for her, she jumped out of bed.

Without waiting to put on the satin robe which her maid had laid over a chair by the bed, she walked in bare feet through the Sitting-Room, guided by the golden light in the distance which led her to the Duke.

When she reached him she saw that he had not called her as she had thought, but was fast asleep, and his face looked very much younger in the light of the candle, which was now burning low.

She stood looking down at him, thinking how

handsome he was and how exactly like his Crusader ancestor on the tomb in the Church.

The day after the wedding, because Yates had insisted that she go out and "take the air," as he put it, before she sat by her unconscious husband, she had walked down the drive thinking that she would look at the flowers in the Church.

It had been impossible to see them at all clearly since there had been so many people present at her marriage.

When she now entered the beautiful grey stone building, which had been erected at the same time as the first house had been built, she had smelt the fragrance of the lilies.

She thought that without the packed congregation rustling and turning their heads and whispering to one another, there was a feeling of faith and sanctity that stretched back through the centuries.

It came, she knew, from the family whose members had worshipped there and the people of the village who had come to God with their troubles, big or small, and their experiences, happy or tragic.

As soon as she walked up the aisle she had seen the tomb of the Crusader, and because in her mind it was linked with the Duke as a Knight, she stood for a long time looking at him, as she thought, carved in stone.

Then, as if the atmosphere of the Church demanded it of her, she went down on her knees and prayed that he would love her.

"I want his love, I want him to love me as I love him," she said, "and although I ought to be content that You have given him to me for my husband, please, God, let him love me a little, just a little, so that we will be happy together, as Papa was with Mama when I was a little girl."

She prayed with an intensity that seemed to vibrate from her towards the Knight on the stone tomb.

Then it seemed in her imagination that the Knight

spoke to her and promised that one day she would win her battle just as he had won his.

Now, looking down at the Duke as he slept, close to her and breathing, Samala felt she must pray again.

Perhaps because they were so near to each other, God would understand even better than He had in the Church how much she needed her husband's love.

Then, as it was what she had always done, she went down on her knees and put her hands together in the age-old attitude of prayer and closed her eyes.

"Please, God, please . . ."

She felt her whole being winging up to the sky, reaching out towards the love she craved, and there was no need to put what she prayed for into words.

At the same time, she knew the vibrations that went from her body towards God were a living force.

Only when she felt as if she had sent her heart and her soul up to the very throne of God in supplication, pleading for the love she needed, did she open her eyes.

The Duke's face was very near to hers and he was looking at her in astonishment.

Chapter Six

*S*amala came in through the front door, and the old Butler hurried forward to say:

"I hope Your Grace had a good walk. 'Tis a lovely day for it."

"It is indeed, Higson," Samala replied.

"But Your Grace must not go too far or do too much," the Butler went on. "Nursing His Grace will have taken a great deal out of you."

Samala smiled.

She realised that Higson was speaking like a Nanny, and that all the older servants in the house treated her in the same way, as if she were a child they must look after, cosset, and prevent from doing too much.

It was such a change, after having to do everything for herself at home, thinking out what was required, and having so many difficulties in getting it, that sometimes she felt she had dropped some years from her life and was back in the Nursery.

"Is His Grace down yet?" she asked.

"He should be coming down at any moment, Your Grace," Higson replied, "and by the side staircase, because that'll be easier for him."

"He must do as little as possible today," Samala said as if she was speaking to herself, and added: "Tomorrow, if His Grace is well enough, we are going riding."

"I know Your Grace'll enjoy that," Higson said, "and there's no-one who sits a horse better than His Grace."

Samala smiled as if this was something of which she was well aware. Then she said:

"I am longing to ride with His Grace tomorrow, but I did not bring a whip with me."

She did not explain that hers was so old and dilapidated that she would have been ashamed to show it amidst the perfection that she found everywhere at Buckhurst Park.

"There's no difficulty about that, Your Grace," Higson said. "There's riding-whips here that Your Grace has probably not seen."

He walked to where under the stairs there was a marble-topped table on which were arranged riding-crops and whips of every description.

Samala gave a little cry at the variety of them. Then, as one seemed to outshine the others, she put out her hand towards it, but Higson said quickly:

"That's the only one Your Grace mustn't use."

"Why not?" Samala asked curiously.

"His Grace brought it back with him from India, where it was given to him, I understand, by a Maharajah."

"From India!" Samala exclaimed.

The whip was thin and wiry, the handle topped with gold in which were encrusted small precious stones.

"I am sure it is too valuable to use," she said with a smile.

"It's not that," Higson replied. "Let me show Your Grace."

He picked it up, and while it looked quite an ordinary whip, he pressed a small button on the gold handle and drew from it, as from a sheath, a long, sharp rapier which looked exceedingly dangerous.

"The Maharajah gave it to His Grace," Higson explained, "as a weapon with which to protect himself when he was out riding in the forests."

Samala saw quite clearly how it could prove an excellent defensive weapon if a cobra dropped down from an overhanging branch, or if the Duke were attacked by some savage animal from the ground.

Higson slipped it back into the sheath and picked up another whip from the table.

"I'm sure this one'd suit Your Grace admirably."

"I am sure it will," Samala replied. "Actually, I never use a whip if I can help it, although it is correct to carry one."

"I'm sure any horse'd want to obey Your Grace without having to be punished to do it," Higson replied, and again there was that protective Nanny-like note in his voice which made Samala smile.

Then she could not wait to find the Duke and sped across the Hall to where she knew they were to sit in his private Sitting-Room.

It was a beautiful room, hung with portraits of the Buckhursts which were some of the most valuable in the whole collection.

But when Samala entered she had eyes only for the Duke, who was sitting in the window in an armchair and looking exceedingly smart in his champagne-coloured pantaloons, cut-away coat and intricately tied high cravat.

She ran across the room to him with an eagerness that made him smile.

"How do you feel?" she asked. "You did not find it too tiring getting dressed and coming downstairs?"

"I feel like my old self," the Duke answered, "and from now on, I will have no more fussing about my health, which I assure you is a word I have grown to dislike!"

"It is to be expected from the people who love you," Samala remarked.

The Duke glanced at her and it flashed through his mind that love to Samala meant something different from what it meant to the women in the past who had told him that they loved him. But it was not a subject he wanted to dwell on at the moment.

"Luncheon will be ready in a minute," Samala said, "then we will decide what you would like to do this afternoon. I have thought, although you may not agree, that you would like to see your new orchids in the Orangery."

"You are quite right," the Duke said, "and I wonder why I did not think of it myself."

"I have been looking at them every day," Samala said, "and hoping they would blossom out into a fantastic display by the time you came to see them! But I am not going to say any more. They are to be a surprise."

The Duke smiled.

"I never realised until you came here," he said, "how many surprises there are in my house, and I expect you have found a number in the gardens."

"I have," Samala agreed. "I could not believe there was a place on earth that was so beautiful and so exquisite. It is like what I think Heaven will be if I ever get there."

The Duke smiled.

"When I first saw you I thought you looked like an angel," he said, "so of course Heaven is your natural habitat."

"Do you really think that?" Samala asked with interest. "Most people say despairingly that I look so young! They seem to forget that sooner or later I am bound to get older."

The Duke laughed.

"That is something that is unfortunately inevitable."

There was silence. Then he asked:

"What is worrying you?"

"I was thinking," Samala said, "that perhaps you were disappointed that I did not look older and more dignified. I always imagined that Duchesses were very tall and very distinguished, and I think if ever I was to wear one of the big Buckhurst tiaras, I would look like a mushroom!"

The Duke laughed as if he could not help himself.

"That is undoubtedly true, so we had better keep to the smaller wreaths and bandeaux, of which I believe there are quite a number."

Samala looked at him. Then she asked:

"You did not notice the one I was wearing at our wedding?"

The Duke thought it best to be honest.

"No. Were you wearing a wreath?"

Samala gave a little sigh.

"I did hope when I drove to the Church with Papa you would think I looked pretty and as you expected your wife to be."

There was a wistful note in her voice that made the Duke say:

"I suppose you might say I was nervous of being married—remember, it was for the first time—or perhaps it is because I have had concussion that I can now remember very little about our wedding."

"For me it was very . . . very . . . wonderful!"

Then, as if she felt he might think she was complaining, she said quickly:

"I will keep my wedding-gown and wear it when you are feeling better so that you can see how lovely it was. Perhaps I could wear it every year on our anniversary, unless I grow too fat."

"I think that is unlikely."

The Duke spoke drily, and she was not certain if it was a compliment or not, but before she could say any more, luncheon was announced.

They ate in what was known as the Small Dining-Room, a very lovely oval room decorated by Robert Adam in his famous leaf green, with alcoves in which there were marble figures of gods.

"When you are sitting here," Samala asked, "do you

sometimes feel as if you are on Olympus and associating with the other gods like yourself?"

The Duke's eyes twinkled.

"You are not elevating me from a Crusader to the majesty of Apollo or Zeus?"

"Apollo, of course," Samala said quickly. "Think how good he was with horses!"

The Duke laughed.

As they went into a spirited discussion on whether the Greek horses were as fine as those bred today in England, he thought when the meal ended that whenever he was with Samala, she always appeared to have new ideas to talk about.

Undoubtedly he would have to use his brain to be able to keep up his end and to answer her questions.

He had already learnt that she not only loved horses and riding but had a most unusual knowledge of horse-breeding and of the hopes which belonged to all the great race-horse owners like himself.

"How can you know so much about Lord Derby's horses?" he asked when they were discussing them at some length.

"It is of course due to Papa," Samala answered. "I am afraid that although he could not really afford it, he read a sporting-paper every day as well as *The Times*."

The Duke thought it was in *The Times* that she had read his speeches, and she must also have studied the sporting-papers from cover to cover to be as knowledge-able as she was on a subject which was especially his own.

"I have already learnt," he said, "that while I have been sleeping you have visited my stables."

"How could I help it?" she asked. "I have never seen such wonderful horses! I have spent a lot of time talking to *Wild Rufus*. I think he has promised me he will never be so rough with you again."

"If you make him too tame I shall be extremely annoyed," the Duke replied.

111

"I do not think he will ever be that," Samala answered seriously, "but I could not . . . bear him to injure you . . . again."

There was a little throb in her voice which the Duke did not miss. At the same time, he decided to ignore it.

He had the uncomfortable feeling that Samala's love for him was growing day by day, and he was afraid that once he was back to living normally again, she would find it hard to adjust herself to not being with him all the time.

'I do not want to hurt her,' he thought. 'At the same time, I have my own life to live, and that is something she will have to accept.'

When luncheon was over, as they walked slowly down the passages to the Orangery, he could feel vibrating from Samala her excitement at what she was going to show him, and he thought it was rather touching.

He had never known a woman he was with to be excited about anything but his own desires for her, and yet, because she wanted to give him pleasure, Samala was, he knew, as thrilled by the orchids that were waiting for his approval as if he were giving her a diamond necklace.

It struck him that it would be interesting to see her reaction to any present he did give her, and he thought he had in fact been very remiss in not remembering that he should have given her one at least on their wedding-day.

Samala opened the doors of the Orangery, which had been built early in the last century and was a fine example of early Georgian architecture.

The sun was shining through the long windows and lighting the flowers which filled the long, narrow building with a profusion of colour and looked very lovely against the background of green palms and other exotic shrubs which the Duke had been experimenting with recently.

There was a small stone fountain playing in the centre of the Orangery, and as they reached it Samala slipped her hand into his, and he saw on one side of the fountain a breathtaking display of the white and pink orchids he had brought from Darjeeling.

They were so small and exquisite as their star-like petals opened to the sun that it inevitably flashed through the Duke's mind that they were exactly like Samala.

It was almost as if when he had found them and brought them back to England he was thinking of her.

His fingers had tightened on hers, and he could feel her excitement and her joy at what he was seeing. He knew also that her blue eyes were watching his face anxiously to be certain of his reaction.

He did not speak, and she asked at length in a low voice:

"You are . . . pleased?"

"Delighted!" he answered. "And I think as they have no name they should be called after you."

Samala gave a little gasp. Then she asked:

"Do you mean that . . . do you really mean it? It is the loveliest present you could give me! Thank you . . . thank you!"

The Duke turned to look at her, and as her face was tipped up to his he had the feeling that because she was happy and pleased by what he had said, she wanted to throw her arms round him and kiss him.

It struck him that this was an appropriate moment at which he should kiss his wife for the first time, but even as he thought of it there was an interruption and he was aware that Higson was approaching them.

"What is it, Higson?" the Duke asked.

"The Baroness von Schlüter has called to see Your Grace," Higson said a little breathlessly. "Her Ladyship says she is in the neighbourhood and is anxious to have a word with Your Grace before she returns to London."

The Duke thought with a twist of his lips that the Baroness's excuse was very obvious.

He was well aware that she had come because, although by this time she must have learnt of his accident, he had not communicated with her as she would have expected.

He was suddenly aware that Samala's fingers had stiffened in his, and he knew she was waiting for the reply he would give Higson.

He knew that she was tense, not because she was afraid or jealous of the Baroness, of whom he was sure she knew nothing, but because she felt that the caller had encroached on the time they were to spend together, and to which she had been looking forward eagerly because it was the first time he had come downstairs.

It flashed through his mind that if he was to see the Baroness, Samala would feel lonely and shut out like a child who having been promised a visit to the Pantomime was disappointed at the last moment.

Even as he thought of it he suddenly realised, and it seemed incredible, that he himself had no wish to see the Baroness at this moment.

It was almost as if she was, in some way which he could not put into words, alien to the house, to the orchids, to the sunshine, and of course to Samala.

For the moment he could not believe what he was feeling was true, and yet he knew positively that the woman who had held him with the fiery passion of desire was not acceptable and he definitely did not wish to see her.

Higson was waiting and so was Samala, and although so many thoughts had passed through his mind, it was only a question of seconds before he said:

"Convey my apologies to the Baroness, Higson, and say that it is with regret that I am still under the Doctor's orders not to receive any visitors for the next few days."

As he spoke he knew that the smile was back on Samala's lips and the sunshine was back in her eyes.

He felt, too, her fingers move, and it was almost as if she gave a little skip of happiness because he would stay with her.

"Very good, Your Grace," Higson said respectfully, and walked back the way he had come.

"And now I want to show you some other orchids," Samala said, "which are very lovely, but not, I shall always think, as beautiful as my . . . own."

She took the Duke round the fountain as she spoke and they looked at the other orchids. Then Samala said firmly that he had done enough walking and must go back to the Sitting-Room.

He did not argue with her, for in fact he felt, to his surprise, as if his legs were somewhat unsteady, and when he reached his comfortable armchair in the window, he sat down in it thankfully.

Almost as if she knew what he was feeling, Samala asked no questions but merely went to the grog-tray in the corner and brought him back a glass of champagne from the inevitable bottle that was open in the wine-cooler.

Higson had explained to her that, extravagant though it might seem, when the Duke was in residence there was always champagne in any room he used.

"Not that His Grace often drinks more than a glass a day," he said, "unlike some gentlemen who come here. But it's part of the hospitality that is traditional at Buckhurst Park, Your Grace, and in any other houses His Grace owns."

"I think it is a lovely idea," Samala said, "and rather like the monks in the Monasteries who feed any wayfarers who come to their door and regard them as being their guests."

"I 'spect it all goes back to some old religion," Higson agreed. "That's the sort of thing, Your Grace, that makes England what it is, but we won't bother about that."

"We will not indeed," Samala agreed.

She thought it was another thing she might have expected from her Crusader that he should be generous with his hospitality in the same way as he would be willing to help in any way anybody who appealed to him.

The Duke took the champagne and sipped it, then found himself thinking how strange it was that he did not at all want to see the Baroness, and how angry she must have been at being turned away from the door.

'She will get over it,' he thought.

Then he realised it did not matter to him particularly whether she got over it or not, and he knew astoundingly that the curtain had fallen on another of his love-dramas.

When he did return to London he would not renew his association with the Baroness von Schlüter.

The Duke was used to his *affaires de coeur* coming to an end almost in some cases before anybody realised they had begun.

When he had left the Baroness he had been so annoyed at having to do so that he had been quite certain that almost immediately after his wedding he would return to her.

The fire she had engendered in him and her expertise in what he himself had always thought of as the Science of Passion were so great that at times the Duke had felt that instead of being the dominant partner in their liaison, he was the pupil.

And yet now—and he could hardly believe it was the truth—the thought of her did not at all make him want to see her again, while the manner in which they had disported themselves seemed in retrospect to be really quite wild and positively embarrassing.

The Duke was very conscious of his own consequence, but that had never intruded upon him before in his intimate moments of making love.

Yet now as he looked at Samala's very young, angelic little face as she sat in the window turning the pages of a book, he thought she must never know of the way women like the Baroness behaved.

What is more, it would be the greatest mistake for her ever to come in contact with her or with any of his other past loves.

He had a feeling that she would not only be shocked by them but also hurt and dismayed that he, the hero to whom she attributed such gallant deeds, should be associated with them.

"I must certainly protect her from that sort of thing," the Duke decided.

Then he thought that was a strange thing for him to determine, and even stranger that he should feel that he wanted to protect a woman not only from other women but from a too intimate knowledge of his past.

He supposed it was because she was so child-like that there was something deeply disturbing in thinking of her being besmirched and despoilt by what he supposed, if he was honest, was both sordid and certainly immoral.

Then he remembered that there was nothing child-like about Samala's brain, and because sometimes he had been aware that intuitively she could read his thoughts, he told himself that he would have to be careful, very, very careful, that he did not despoil her in any way.

He knew that to do so would be like tearing to pieces and stamping into the ground his star-like orchids, and once again he was thinking of the sunshine on her hair and the translucence of her skin.

She might have dropped straight out of Heaven or from some twinkling star onto the window-seat in front of him.

It suddenly struck him that to kiss her, to touch her, and to teach her about love would be very different from anything he had ever done before.

Now that he thought about it, he could not remember that he had ever made love to a woman who was completely innocent and—as he had demanded of his wife—untouched.

It was quite unnecessary for him to ask Samala if any man had ever kissed her.

He knew that the purity he had felt vibrating from her, and which he had seen in her face when he found her praying beside his bed, came not only from what she thought and what she knew but from her very soul.

It was something which the Duke had not thought about since he was at School and had been obliged to attend Chapel twice a day.

Then he had dismissed it as a somewhat dubious idea about a part of a person which could not be proved to exist.

But now he thought that Samala's soul was a very real part of herself, and it was another thing he must protect. It was all part of his duty because she belonged to him.

Then, as if inevitably his thoughts communicated themselves to Samala, she raised her eyes, and when they met the Duke's it was somehow impossible for either of them to look away.

* * *

By the time they had had tea together, on which the Chef had made a tremendous effort with cakes of every description, including some that were iced and decorated with cherries and crystalised violets, the Duke was feeling tired.

He had enjoyed not only the tea but watching Samala exclaiming over the cakes and the tiny sandwiches, which she had eaten with the appetite of a child at a party.

"Mama used to explain to me that people who lived in big houses ate like this, but it was something we could not afford to do at home."

"What did you have to eat?" the Duke asked.

"Only bread and butter to begin with," Samala

replied, "then there was a choice of honey which came from our own bees, or jam which we made in the summer and which was sometimes rather bitter because we could not afford enough sugar."

"How can you possibly have been so poor?" the Duke asked somewhat sceptically.

"Papa used to ask the same question," Samala answered. "First of all, the war upset everything, and the farmers had no money and no young men to work the land properly, which meant that they could not pay their rent."

She sighed, then went on:

"But of course Papa could not turn them out, and so they stayed on and paid nothing, but that meant that we had nothing either."

"But your father must have had some other income?"

"My grandfather was very extravagant. He did leave a few shares, besides his debts, but unfortunately they were in Companies which did not pay or went bankrupt, and there were Bonds which Papa said were not worth the paper they were written on."

"It is certainly a very sad story," the Duke said, "but now it is all over, and I hope I will be able to help your father in some way which will not make him feel he is under an obligation to me."

"Could you do that?" Samala asked. "It would be very wonderful, because I know that Papa will always feel that he should not have married a woman richer than himself."

She had already told the Duke how she had contrived to make her father marry Maureen Henley before she left him.

Because she had told the story in an amusing way she had made him laugh, even though he had been perceptive enough to realise that Samala had been desperately worried about leaving her father with nobody to look after him and without even the means of feeding himself properly.

"I have not thought it out yet," the Duke went on, "but perhaps I could suggest to your father that because I intend to expand my breeding of mares very considerably in the next few years, I would like to rent some land from him, and that would mean I could keep it in good trim, reseed it, and perhaps even take over one of his farms."

Samala clasped her hands together and said:

"Could you really do that without Papa thinking you were being charitable?"

"I assure you I am well known for my tact in matters of that sort."

"I am sure you are!" Samala exclaimed. "But how can you be so marvellous and so kind as to think of something that would make Papa happy and rich again?"

"I want to make you happy," the Duke said in his deep voice.

"That is what I want to make you."

She jumped off the window-seat to kneel beside his chair.

"Please . . . please . . . get well quickly," she pleaded. "Then we can ride over the boundary and I will show you exactly the place where you could turn out your mares with their foals, and there is a derelict farm that only wants repairing."

The Duke put out his hand to touch her hair.

It felt just as he had expected it would—soft, silky, and yet somehow vibrant, as if it had a life of its own.

"I am well!" he said. "If it would be too long a ride tomorrow, we will definitely try to do it the next day, or the day after that."

He heard Samala draw in her breath. Then as his hand dropped from her hair she bent forward and kissed it.

* * *

Having gone up to bed early after dinner, pretending to himself that he was doing so to please Samala, but really because he was beginning to feel very tired, the Duke awoke feeling different in every way and knowing that he was almost back to his old vitality and inevitably in need of exercise.

He had eaten a good breakfast in the Sitting-Room and wondered why Samala had not come to join him, until he learnt that she was already dressed and had gone down to the stables to consult with his Head Groom as to which horse he should ride.

Just for a moment the Duke thought it rather irritating that he was not even allowed to make his own choice.

Then he knew that Samala was only thinking of him, being aware that a horse that pulled violently would be very tiring for him on his first day on horseback.

Although none of his horses was tame and docile, it was not for the moment wise for him to ride anything as spirited as *Wild Rufus*.

"I suppose," he said almost grudgingly, "she was thinking of me."

He spoke the words aloud, without realising that Yates was there, and he answered:

"There's never been a lady, Your Grace, who's thought of you as Her Grace does, and Your Grace knows I'm speaking the truth."

"I thought quite a lot of ladies have thought about me in one way or another," the Duke remarked cynically.

"But they've not been like Her Grace," Yates persisted. "Mr. Higson was saying only yesterday that it's as if ever since Her Grace came here the sunshine has come into the house, and there's a new feeling about the place that wasn't here before."

"What on earth do you mean by that?" the Duke enquired.

He was used to Yates expressing things in his own

way, and because he had been with him for so long, the Duke found the little man rather amusing, and often listened to him as he would not have listened to any of his other servants.

"Well, it's like this, Your Grace," Yates said. "As you asks me, Her Grace is different because her heart's in the right place, and she's good through and through."

He paused for a moment, then went on:

"It's not only because she has a kind word for everybody she meets, and a smile that makes you smile back whether you wants to or not, but it's just that she seems to give us all something, and it's something we wanted, even if we didn't know it."

The Duke looked at him in astonishment, and Yates scratched his head as he said:

"I 'opes I'm explaining it right, Your Grace, but that's what I feels, and there's a great number round 'ere as feels the same."

Then Yates, as if he was embarrassed by his own oratory, walked from the Sitting-Room into the bed-room.

The Duke stared after him in amazement.

Then he thought strangely that it was what he had been thinking himself, and although he had no wish to admit it, that was what Samala had given him.

Lying on the breakfast-table were letters from both his sisters, but he did not open them, having the feeling that they had written to him more out of curiosity than for any other reason.

He knew that Elizabeth had been in touch not only with the Doctor but also with Samala and had made extensive enquiries about his health.

He was astute enough to know that what really interested her was how he was progressing with his marriage.

She would be yearning to know whether or not his gloomy forebodings had been swept away by Samala's charm, or if she was making his convalescence a long period of unendurable boredom.

But that was something about which he had no intention of talking. If his sisters were curious, he thought, they could damn well go on being curious, as they had always been about him in the past.

What he thought about Samala was his business and his business alone, and he had no intention of being pressured by his sisters or anybody else to talk about his private affairs until he was ready to do so.

Then, because he knew Samala would be waiting for him, he started to dress himself, with Yates's help, and knew he was looking forward to riding with an eagerness he used to feel on his first day home from Eton.

When finally he came down the Grand Staircase, the footmen in the Hall looked at him admiringly.

They were well aware there was nobody to equal their Master in his appearance in the sporting-field and in the manner in which he rode the horses he owned.

As the Duke reached the Hall, Samala came hurrying through the front door, and he saw how the extremely attractive blue habit she wore accentuated the blue of her eyes and was echoed by the gauze veil which encircled her high-crowned riding-hat.

"The horses are outside," she said breathlessly, "and I do hope you will be pleased that we thought *Crusader* would suit you best."

The Duke was aware by the way she spoke that it was not only because she thought *Crusader* would suit him but also because the name was most appropriate for the first occasion on which they would ride together.

Crusader was in fact a black stallion very much like the one he had been riding the first time Samala had seen him, when he won the Steeple-Chase.

He knew without her telling him that all this had passed through her mind, and that at the same time she was afraid he would not understand and would spoil what was a very special occasion for her by having different ideas.

He had no idea why he was so perceptive about Samala's thoughts and feelings, yet he knew he was, and he saw her eyes light up like stars and a radiant smile curve her lips when he said exactly what she wanted to hear.

"I am delighted to ride *Crusader*," he said, "and I only hope you have chosen a horse for yourself that will keep up with him."

"Of course I have!"

She paused. Then she said:

"I am riding *White Knight*."

The Duke gave a little laugh because the choice was so obvious. Yet, he thought it was all part of the fairy-story, and he would not do anything to spoil it.

"Let us set off together," he suggested, and started to walk down the steps.

He was not allowed to do that alone, and Yates was ready for him to put a hand on his shoulder.

Samala took two steps after them before she suddenly turned and ran back into the Hall.

She had forgotten her whip, and she was just about to tell Higson so, when she realised that he was outside on the steps, watching his Master's descent and ready to go to his other side should he be required.

Without waiting to tell a footman to bring it to her, she ran under the stairs and picked up what she thought was the whip which Higson had recommended to her.

Only when the Duke was already in the saddle and the Head Groom had assisted her onto the back of *White Knight* did she realise that she had not brought the ordinary riding-whip with her, but the special one with the jewelled top which had come from India.

For a moment she thought she should change it, then she told herself it would only delay the Duke, and was quite unnecessary, as she was unlikely to need to use it on *White Knight,* who was already moving restlessly as if anxious to be off.

Quickly she moved him level with the Duke, and as they rode away everybody was watching them, thinking what a picture they made.

The Duke was magnificent on the black stallion, and Samala, small, fragile, and seemingly too delicate to control *White Knight,* and yet she was riding, as the Head Groom said beneath his breath: "As if her were the spitting image of His Grace!"

They reached the bridge over the lake before the Duke said:

"Now I am going to take you somewhere which I am sure you have not discovered. It is a very special place which I always visit my first day when I come home."

"Tell me about it," Samala said eagerly.

"It is another lake which is through some woods at the bottom end of the Park, where there are many species of wild duck and other birds which you will not see anywhere else on the Estate."

"How exciting!" Samala exclaimed. "I am glad I have not seen it before, and it will be very, very special to see it with you."

"I thought you would think that," the Duke answered. "We can now ride quite quickly along to the bottom of the Park, but when we get to the wood we have to go in single file down a narrow ride, and I will lead the way."

"Of course," Samala said, "and when we reach your secret lake we must have a competition to see who can recognise the most birds."

She gave a little sigh.

"I am sure you will win. At the same time, I want to try to beat you."

"It will be very humiliating if you do," the Duke said, "because, as I have already said, since nobody else has ever been interested in it, I have always felt it is my special lake and belongs especially to me."

Then, as if he felt he was shutting her out, he said:
"But now of course I will share it with you."

"Not if you do not want to," Samala said quickly.

"You cannot have forgotten," the Duke said, "that at
the Marriage Service I said distinctly that 'with all my
worldly goods I thee endow,' and that certainly includes
my secret lake."

She gave him a smile that showed her dimples very
clearly. Then she said:

"One day I will think of something I can give you,
but as I own no worldly goods, it will have to be
something very, very special that comes from the heavenly spheres."

"That is certainly an idea," the Duke said, "and I
shall look forward to receiving it."

Then as they crossed the bridge and *Crusader*
indicated that this was no time for conversation, the
Duke relaxed his hold on the reins and they were
moving swiftly along the bottom of the Park towards the
wood in the far distance.

Chapter Seven

*R*iding with the Duke, Samala thought it was the most exciting thing she had ever done in her whole life.

Sometimes in her dreams she had imagined that they were riding together, but since he was a Knight in armour, she had felt that she herself did not quite fit into the picture.

Yet, it had been a thrill that she translated into her stories when she was awake, and she hoped each night that the dream would be repeated, so that she and her Knight would be together.

But now she was actually with him, and it was even more wonderful than she had imagined it would be.

Despite the fact that she was mainly concerned with keeping *White Knight* under control, she kept glancing at the Duke and thinking that no man could look more magnificent or exactly as she had imagined he would be.

She loved the way he wore his tall hat a little to one side of his dark head.

Although she thought when he was actually mounting his horse he had suffered a little pain from the bruise on his chest, now that he was in the saddle he appeared to have forgotten it.

Crusader, whom she had made a great fuss of in the stables, not only because of his name but also because he was one of the Duke's most outstanding horses, looked exactly as if he had stepped out of a painting, and the same might have been said of the Duke himself.

When Samala put on her blue riding-habit she had hoped that the Duke would think she looked no less smart and attractive than the dozens of other ladies with whom he must have ridden.

No-one had spoken to her of the Duke's past or of the women there must have been in his life, but Samala was too intelligent not to know there must have been many of them and that they had loved him to distraction because he was so handsome.

It had astonished her that he had not been married until now, and once again she was saying a little prayer of gratitude because he had chosen her to be his wife.

"How can I make him happy?" she asked, as she had asked the same question hundreds of times every night.

But she knew, marvellous though it was to be with the Duke, that there was something missing in their relationship, and that if she was honest, it was love.

She loved him, and every moment of every day that she was with him her love grew until it filled the world.

She thought sometimes that she could feel her whole being reaching out towards him, giving him the love which she could feel in her heart, her mind, and her body.

She had always known that love would be like this, overwhelming, irresistible, and a rapture like the sunshine and the music she had heard on the wind.

"That is what I feel about him," she said to herself in the darkness, "but why should he feel the same about me?"

Because she was so unselfconscious about herself, Samala was very modest and humble.

The years of being poor and having to struggle at the Priory had taught her never to think of herself but only of her father and the house.

Now, when she had no material worries as to where

the next meal was coming from or whether the mice were eating their way through the wainscotting, she had time to think about somebody called "Samala," who seemed almost a stranger.

When she looked at herself in the mirror she could hardly believe that the very elegantly gowned reflection she saw was her own.

Because she had had so much more to eat and time to enjoy it, the dark little lines under her eyes had disappeared, and she thought that the line of her chin was not so sharp and her breasts had grown a little fuller.

It made her, although she did not think of it that way, look even younger and more angelic than she had before.

She had no idea that when she looked at the Duke with love, there seemed to be a light burning within her, which shone in her eyes and created an aura round her that to anyone with perception was inescapable.

It was because she was happy and in love that the servants found her like a ray of sunshine, and she found everything she looked at so entrancing that she wanted to share it with other people, but most of all with the Duke.

She would wake in the morning trying to think of new things that would interest him, subjects they could discuss and questions she could ask him because he was so wise that she wanted to learn from him.

"He is wonderful . . . so wonderful!" she told herself a dozen times a day.

Now she was saying it again, and it was as if it was in time to the rhythm of the horses' hoofs.

"He is wonderful, and there is no-one in the world like him!"

As if he was aware of her feelings, he turned his head to smile at her, and she felt her heart turn over in her breast.

"Enjoying yourself?" he asked.

"So much that I have no words to express it."

"I too am enjoying being back in the saddle."

"I thought you would feel like that."

He smiled at her again, and without really thinking about it she edged *White Knight* a little nearer to him.

The wood was not far ahead and the Duke drew *Crusader* to a trot, then to a walk.

"You see the trees?" he said. "That is where we are going. Next year I intend to thin them out, so that it will be easier to reach the lake."

"You must not make it too easy," Samala said, "otherwise there will be people who will find their way there besides us."

"I thought that myself," the Duke said. "Perhaps that is the reason why I have left the wood as it is for so long."

Samala liked the way he was talking, as if he was sharing with her his care and concern for the Estate.

She knew it was something she wanted him to share with her in the future, just as her father had done.

But with the Priory it had been a long tale of frustration and misery because it was impossible to make any of the improvements which were long overdue.

However, she felt sure that Maureen would understand his difficulties, and besides restoring the house as she was longing to do, she would also understand how every tree, every hedge, every field of the Estate meant something very close and personal to her father.

"Why are you looking so serious?" the Duke asked suddenly.

"I was thinking about Papa, and hoping my new Stepmother will help him with the Estate, which is in such a lamentable state of disrepair."

"I thought you and I were going to improve that."

He saw Samala's eyes shine as if a thousand candles had been lit inside them, and as if he was afraid she was going to thank him he said:

"We will talk about that tomorrow. Now, all you have to concentrate on is my secret lake. If we approach it quietly we will not disturb the birds before you have a chance to see them."

He went ahead as he spoke, and Samala thought it was a mistake to speak.

The wood of close-set fir trees was, as he had said, overgrown, and they now entered a very narrow ride which had once been wider.

There was only room for one horse to go along it at a time, and Samala therefore dropped behind him on *White Knight*.

Because she loved the Duke she felt as if the trees were speaking to her, and the pigeons that flew off at their approach seemed not to be frightened but only showing off the beauty of their plumage as they soared above the tree-tops.

The sun percolated only faintly through the thick branches, making a golden pattern on the sandy ground. Samala thought that, like everything else connected with the Duke, the wood was beautiful and unusual, and her imagination immediately began to turn it into a fantasy.

The Duke rode on, and they must have ridden almost into the centre of the wood, when suddenly from right and left of her there sprang two men.

Their appearance was so unexpected that Samala started and instinctively tightened her rein on *White Knight*.

As she did so, to her horror the man on the Duke's left seized hold of his arm and started to drag him from his horse's back.

For a second she could not grasp what was happening. Then as the Duke resisted and *Crusader* reared up, the other man hit the stallion with a bludgeon which he held in his hand.

The Duke was pulled to the ground and the horse galloped off wildly down the ride, the stirrups rocking loosely at his sides.

As the Duke reached the ground he fought himself free of the man who was holding him and started to fight him with a clenched right fist, at the same time holding off the blows from the bludgeon with his riding-whip.

It was then, almost as if she were in a nightmare of horror, that Samala realised that the second man, who had been separated from the Duke by *Crusader*, was now about to strike him with the heavy bludgeon he was wielding in both hands.

The Duke had his back to him, and as the man swung the bludgeon over his shoulder Samala acted.

Without even thinking about it, almost as if a power outside herself told her what to do, she rode *White Knight* forward and drew the rapier clear of its sheath in the handle of the riding-whip.

It was not a question of timing, just instinct, and as *White Knight*, urged on by her spur, swept between the man and the Duke, she bent forward and thrust the point of the rapier between his shoulder and neck.

He gave a hoarse cry which echoed out in the wood.

For a split second the other man took his eyes off the Duke to see what had happened, and the Duke, with the skill of an accomplished pugilist, struck him with his right fist on the point of the chin and knocked him senseless.

It took Samala all her strength to pull in *White Knight*, but she managed it, and then turned back.

Only as she did so did she realise that the Duke was standing in the centre of the track, where the two men who had attacked him were lying senseless on either side of him.

She reached him, and only as she pulled in *White Knight* did she realise how frightened she was and that she was trembling so violently that it was hard to keep in the saddle.

The Duke looked up at her and said:

"I am afraid you will have to give me a lift, as there is no question of catching *Crusader*."

He spoke quite calmly, as if nothing unusual had

occurred, and in contrast Samala's voice was very low and frightened as she asked:

"You . . . are all . . . right? Those terrible men have . . . not hurt . . . you?"

"I am all right," the Duke replied, "but I think we should get away from here."

As he spoke he reached out towards her saddle, and as she understood what he was about to do, she took her foot out of the stirrup so that he could put his into it.

He swung himself up behind her and she moved forward as far as she could, thinking it was fortunate that she was so small and the saddle was a large one.

As he put his arms round her and took the reins from her, the Duke was aware that her whole body was trembling.

Because Samala felt rather faint, she put up her hand and pulled her riding-hat from her head so that it was easier to lean back against the Duke's shoulder.

She remembered it was what she had done as a child when her father had often carried her on the front of his saddle.

Moving slowly and carefully down the ride, the Duke did not even look back at the men they had left lying on the ground, and only when it was possible to speak did Samala say in a voice he could barely hear:

"D-did I . . . kill that . . . man?"

"I hope so," the Duke replied, "but do not worry. Leave everything to me. I do not intend that you shall be involved in this."

"B-but . . . I am . . . involved."

"No!" he said sharply. "That is something I will not allow."

She did not understand, but she felt too faint to argue, knowing that it might have been the Duke who was lying on the ground.

She had seen a bludgeon before, and she knew that what each of the men had carried was a stick with a bulbous and heavy head to it, with a great number of nails driven into the wood.

Her father had told her how bludgeons were carried by footpads and robbers, and if a man was hit squarely on the head with one it could kill him.

She knew now, although it had all happened too quickly even for thought, that that was what would have happened if the second man had struck the Duke on the head as he was preparing to do.

'I saved him!' she thought.

Yet, the screams of the man she had struck with the rapier seemed still to ring in her ears, and she knew that when she had ridden back to pick up the Duke she had seen a crimson flood of blood over the rough handkerchief he wore round his neck.

Now they were free of the trees and the Duke was riding a little faster, and when the house was in sight, he said:

"I want you to go straight upstairs to your room, Samala, and lie down. You are not to talk to anybody about what has occurred, but rest until I come to you."

"I . . . I was afraid . . . very afraid that he might . . . kill you."

"I know," the Duke answered. "You saved my life, and we will talk about it later. Now I want you to do exactly what I have told you."

They were moving along the bottom of the Park, when as they reached the drive they saw ahead of them a string of horses being exercised by the stable-boys, heading in the opposite direction to the one the Duke and Samala had taken.

He called out to them and they stopped to stare in astonishment at seeing their Master and his wife on one horse.

The Duke rode up to them.

"Four of you," he said authoritatively, "go at once down the ride in the wood, where you will find two footpads. They are unconscious, but tie them up so that they cannot escape, and keep guard over them until I send a brake to collect them."

The boys appeared to understand, but they did not reply, and the Duke went on:

"You, Jed, are to ride to the Chief Constable's house. I expect you know where it is."

"Yes, Yer Grace."

"Then hurry across country. Ask him to come here as quickly as possible to see me, and tell him it is urgent."

Jed touched his cap and, without waiting, set off at a gallop.

"One of you go through the wood and look for *Crusader* by the lake," the Duke said to the other young men, "and the rest of you continue to exercise the horses as you intended to do."

With that he rode past them down the drive towards the house.

He pulled *White Knight* to a standstill at the bottom of the steps and said to Samala:

"Do exactly as I told you, and do not worry."

"You . . . are all . . . right?" she asked in the voice of a child who wishes to be reassured.

"I shall be all right," he said with a smile. "Just trust me, and try to rest."

She gave a little sigh, and it was hard to leave him because the closeness and strength of his arms round her had made her feel safe.

Then, because he was waiting and a footman had hurried down the steps to assist her, Samala slipped her knee over the pummel and slid down to the ground, feeling for a moment as if her feet would not carry her any farther.

Then with an effort she started to walk up the steps as the Duke turned *White Knight* and rode off in the direction of the stables.

She knew as she went through the Hall that Higson

was longing to ask her what had happened and why they had returned without the Duke's horse.

But it was impossible for her to speak, impossible to do anything but carry out the Duke's orders and reach her bedroom.

Her maid was there, a sensible, elderly woman who saw by Samala's pale face and the way her hands were trembling that something had upset her.

Without talking, she helped her take off her riding-habit, brought her a pretty nightgown trimmed with lace, and turned down the bed.

Because she was still feeling faint and shaken by what had happened, Samala slipped between the sheets as if she moved in a dream, and lay back against the pillows.

"Perhaps Your Grace would like something to drink?" the maid asked.

"I think . . . that would . . . be a . . . good idea," Samala replied.

The maid hurried away to come back with a glass of hot milk which was sweetened with honey.

Because she knew it was the sensible thing to do, Samala drank a little of it. Then she lay back again, waiting and longing to know what was happening, aware that she was tense and still very frightened.

It seemed impossible that anything so horrible should have occurred on what she had thought was the happiest day she had ever known.

All she could think of was the danger the Duke had been in and that she had killed a man to save him.

"Why should anybody want to kill or injure him?" she asked, and could find no answer except that the footpads, if that was what they were, wished to steal from him.

The Duke, however, knew the answer very clearly.

He was determined to substantiate his suspicions and to use the man whom he had knocked unconscious and the other, if he was still alive, as evidence against his cousin Edmund.

He had thought once or twice while he was convalescing from his concussion that Edmund might not take his marriage lying down, although he had never envisaged anything so criminal as an attack on him on his own ground.

He had thought that Edmund's fury at his marriage, and the fact that he was deeply in debt, might perhaps result in his taking some desperate action with which he would have to deal forcibly.

As he gave orders for the brake to be sent immediately to the wood to bring the two men back to the stables, where they could be kept prisoner until the arrival of the Chief Constable, he told himself that this was something which must be dealt with once and for all.

Riding back from the wood, he had been at first deeply concerned with the effect that it had had on Samala.

Then as he felt her tremble in his arms and when she had put her head against his shoulder, he knew that she was feeling faint and he must look after her.

As they rode on, the full realisation of how she had saved his life made him understand not only how brave she was but how quick-witted.

He was sure that no other woman he had ever known would have behaved in the same way in such extraordinary circumstances.

Any other would certainly now be screaming and crying hysterically.

'She is behaving as I would like my wife to behave,' he thought.

It was at that moment that he knew, almost as if it was written in front of him in letters of fire, that he loved her.

He could at first hardly believe that the feeling that swept over him was not just the reaction of relief that she had saved him, and surprise that, being so small and frail, she could have done anything as drastic as kill a man in his defence.

Yet he knew that what he now felt for her was what he had been fighting against admitting to himself for the last few days.

She was the white and pink orchid with which he associated her. She was pure and very young. When he least expected it, she had crept into his heart and had filled a place in it which had never been taken by any other woman.

"How can she be so unique?" he asked himself.

He felt the blood throbbing in his temples, and his body pulsating with desire because she was close to him. But it was so much more than what he had felt for a woman dozens of times in the past.

It was something so overwhelming, so tremendous, that he could hardly believe it himself. Yet it was indisputably there, and it was love as he had envisaged it and sought when he was young and idealistic.

It was love as the artists had portrayed it, as the musicians composed it, as the poets wrote of it. It was the love of Romeo and Juliet, Dante and Beatrice, and the Troubadours of Provence.

"It cannot be true!" the Duke argued to himself.

But he knew it was, because although Samala was a woman she was different from any other woman he had ever known before.

He knew as he rode towards the house that Yates was right when he had said she gave everybody something they wanted but had no idea what it was until they received it from her.

'It is love,' the Duke thought.

He wanted to mock at himself for being sentimentally romantic, while at the same time he knew that was what he was feeling.

It was love which had invaded his mind, his heart, and his body, and he was aware that for a very long time he had wanted to kiss Samala.

He had restrained himself from doing so simply because of his prejudice against being married, and also because something fastidious in him as a perfectionist was waiting for the right moment.

But now he thought that except for her courage, the right moment might never have come, and he could have been lying dead on the ride while Edmund became the fifth Duke of Buckhurst.

"You are different from anybody in the whole world," he told Samala silently, "and you are what I have been looking for all my life, although I was not aware of it."

But he knew that for the moment he must protect her, and that whatever happened she must not be involved in the mess that Edmund had created.

When he sent her into the house and rode towards the stables, he was planning to himself exactly how he would explain what had happened. He was determined to make it plausible and ensure that Samala should not be in any way implicated.

He told his version first to his Head Groom and several other members of the stable staff, who all listened with gasps of horror.

"I was attacked by two footpads," he said, "who were waiting for me in the ride in the North Wood. Fortunately, I had discovered soon after we left the house that Her Grace had taken with her as a riding-whip the one I brought back from India which had a rapier concealed in the handle."

As he spoke, he knew it was a weapon they had previously seen or heard about, and he went on:

"I thought it might be dangerous for Her Grace to use that whip in case the catch slipped loose, and I was just about to attach it to my own saddle when two men came out of the trees on either side of the ride to attack me."

His audience drew in their breath and he continued:

"I managed to fend off the first man, and I struck at the second with the rapier, which entered his neck. I then dismounted from *Crusader*, who galloped off as I knocked the first man to the ground."

The way he described it was, he knew, exactly what the men listening to him would expect, and he saw by the admiration in their eyes that he had convinced them that his account was the truth.

After sending the brake to collect the two men, he went back to the house to await the arrival of the Chief Constable.

Fortunately, Colonel Stoner was an old friend whom he had known all his life, and when he heard what had occurred he immediately agreed that the miscreants must be interrogated.

"It is imperative to find out who is behind this attack," he said firmly, "and who has paid them."

After the Duke had given to Colonel Stoner his account of what had happened, they walked to the stables, where the men had by now been brought back from the wood and were imprisoned in one of the empty stalls.

Their legs and arms were bound tightly so that there was no chance of their escaping.

The man whom Samala had stabbed in fact was undoubtedly dead, and the other one was frightened to the point where to save his own skin he was only too ready to talk and explain that he was only carrying out the instructions of the gentleman who had paid him.

The ten guineas they had each been paid were in their pockets, and not only the position of the house, but also a rough map of how they could reach the ride in the wood from the Stage-Coach on which they had travelled, was drawn on a crumpled, dirty piece of paper.

The instructions were in Edmund's handwriting, and there was really no need for the prisoner to give a quite easily recognisable description of him.

When the Chief Constable returned to the house

with the Duke, he suggested that the charge against the man who was alive should be one of robbery with violence, which would be punished by transportation.

Edmund's name would not be brought up at the trial, but the Chief Constable would on the Duke's behalf go to London and insist that he and his wife leave the country immediately, otherwise they would be arrested and charged with conspiracy to murder.

"Will you really do that for me?" the Duke asked.

"Quite frankly," the Chief Constable replied, "I think that after suffering concussion you are not fit to undertake the journey, and you should stay here and look after your wife."

He smiled before he added:

"After all, you are on your honeymoon, and you have not had much chance to enjoy it until now."

"That is true," the Duke agreed.

He saw the Chief Constable glance at the champagne, and as he rose to pour him out a glass, he said:

"Will you make it absolutely clear to Edmund—you have known him as long as you have known me, so perhaps he will listen to you—that I will give him an allowance of two thousand pounds a year, as long as he stays abroad?"

"I will make it even clearer," the Chief Constable replied, "and inform him that if he puts one foot in this country again he will be arrested."

The Duke gave a sigh of relief before he said:

"Actually, I was thinking of how much it would worry my wife if she thought Edmund was always plotting to be rid of me in order to become the next Duke of Buckhurst."

"I will make sure that never happens," the Chief Constable said. "I have heard a great deal about Edmund lately, which I have not troubled to tell you, but which, if you knew of it, would upset you more than you are already."

"Nothing would surprise me," the Duke replied.

"Edmund has been a problem ever since he was a child, and you know what my father thought about him."

"I do indeed," the Chief Constable answered. "Just leave everything in my hands. I promise you this sort of thing will not happen again, and I will see that Edmund and his wife are out of England within the next twenty-four hours."

"Thank you, Colonel," the Duke said simply. "And now, as it is luncheon-time, I hope you will have a meal with me."

"I will, if we can eat quickly," Colonel Stoner replied. "Then I will be on my way to London, and it will save time if I do not return home."

The Duke went from the room to give orders because he also wanted to tell Higson that Her Grace was to have luncheon upstairs and was to be told that he would join her as soon as possible.

* * *

When Samala received the message, she felt desperately disappointed.

As well as riding with the Duke that morning, she had looked forward to having luncheon with him again in the Small Dining-Room with the Greek gods and goddesses watching them.

Then as she tried to eat the luncheon that was brought up to her, she kept worrying in case the Duke was feeling overtired, and she sent her maid to fetch Yates.

He came into the room with a look of concern on his face.

"Your Grace's all right?" he asked.

"I am quite all right," Samala replied, "but I am worried that His Grace is doing too much on his first day up. Please persuade him when the Chief Constable has left to come upstairs and lie down."

"I'll see that he does that, Your Grace," Yates said. "I think, if you asks me, His Grace'll be feeling a bit stiff after his first ride since his wedding-day."

142

He made Samala a little happier about the Duke, though she still could not help worrying.

When her luncheon-tray had been taken from her room, she felt so restless that she got out of bed and walked to the window.

The sun was shining on the lake and the Park looked very quiet and peaceful.

It seemed extraordinary that they should have passed through such a traumatic experience and that in the midst of such beauty there should have been the threat of death.

"Thank You . . . thank You . . . God . . . for helping me to . . . save him," Samala prayed.

Then the horror that she might have failed to do so swept over her, and because it was so terrifying she felt herself tremble and the trees and the sunshine seemed to swim before her eyes.

She heard the door of the Sitting-Room open and she thought it might be her maid or Yates.

Then her instinct told her it was somebody else, and she turned round with a little cry to see the Duke come into the room.

Without thinking, simply because her terror about what had occurred was still with her, she ran towards him and flung herself against him.

"You . . . are safe . . . you are . . . safe! Promise me that will . . . never happen to you . . . again! I do not . . . think I could . . . bear it!"

Her words seemed to fall over one another. Her hands had reached up towards the Duke's neck, and as he put his arms round her she held on to him frantically, as if she was afraid she might lose him.

He looked down at her for a long moment, her eyes misty with tears, her lips trembling, her fair hair tumbled round her cheeks, and he thought no-one could be lovelier, more angelic, or so different.

Then his lips came down on hers.

For a moment Samala could not believe it was happening.

Then as the Duke's arms tightened and his lips became more insistent and demanding, she knew that this was what she had been longing for, this was what she had prayed might happen.

Her feelings of anxiety and terror vanished, and instead the sunshine seemed to invade her body and move upwards through her breasts and into her throat.

She felt as if it carried her love towards the Duke and became a part of him.

He kissed her until she felt as if he drew first her heart, then her soul from between her lips, and she was no longer herself but his.

A long time later the Duke raised his head and said:

"My darling, my sweet! How can you have been so brave as to save my life in the way you did? How can I tell you how glad I am to be alive?"

"I love . . . you!"

Her words were almost inaudible, but the Duke heard them.

Then he was kissing her again, kissing her until Samala felt she must have died and he had carried her into a Heaven where there were only flowers and music and love.

Then, as if the feeling was too great to bear, she made an inarticulate little murmur and hid her face against him.

As she did so, she realised that he was not wearing his riding-clothes as she had expected.

He had undressed and was wearing the long velvet robe she recognised because he had worn it when he had first been allowed out of bed to sit in an armchair in his room.

"You are . . . going to . . . rest?" she asked, and her voice seemed to be unsteady and to come from a long distance.

"That is what I told you to do," the Duke replied,

"and I think it would be sensible, my precious, if it was something we both did."

Before she could answer him, he picked her up in his arms and carried her to her bed, and laid her down against the pillows.

Then he went to the door, locked it, and came back to stand beside her to say:

"I have so much to tell you, and I know it is what you are longing to hear. So shall I rest with you?"

He saw the light in her eyes and did not wait for her answer, but went round the other side of the bed, and taking off his robe got in beside her, thinking as he did so that the cupids and love-knots were very appropriate.

Samala's eyes watched him, then as he turned towards her and put his arm round her she whispered:

"When you . . . kissed me it was the most . . . wonderful perfect thing that has ever . . . happened to me . . . I thought I must have . . . died . . . or have been dreaming."

"I want to teach you about love, my darling."

"Are you . . . saying that you . . . love me?"

"Of course I love you!" he answered. "I feel as if I have loved you for a thousand years! Perhaps that is true, and we have only just found each other again."

Samala drew in her breath.

"I have felt like . . . that ever since I first saw you looking like a Knight," she said, "and now I am sure you are . . . right and we have . . . loved each other for a . . . million centuries . . . and now we are together . . . forever and . . . ever."

There was a little pause before she spoke the last two words, as if it was a question, and the Duke said with a smile:

"Forever and eternity, my precious. I know now that you are what I want in my life, a little angel who will guide me and help me and who also has a very special place in my heart, where I will always worship her."

Samala gave a cry. Then she said:

"You cannot . . . really be saying . . . this to me! I must be . . . dreaming!"

The Duke laughed.

"If you are, then I am dreaming too, and let me say it is a very exciting dream."

As he spoke he kissed her eyes, her small turned-up nose, and the two dimples on either side of her mouth, which he had watched for from the first moment he had really looked at her.

Then, only when he knew that Samala's lips were parted and waiting for his, did he kiss the line of her chin, the softness of her neck, then finally his mouth was on hers.

As he felt her quiver against him, he knew it was just as thrilling and as ecstatic as he had thought it would be to awaken her to the realisation that she was a woman.

Then the Duke was feeling sensations he had never known before and which were very different from those he had experienced in his numerous love-affairs.

They were not only physically wildly exciting, but at the same time spiritually uplifting and ecstatic, and he kissed Samala until he was aware that the fire burning within himself had ignited a tiny flame within her.

He knew from long experience that he must be gentle and very controlled and nothing he did must frighten her or destroy the trust she had given him.

This was very much a part of their love, and it was also, although the Duke felt shy of the word, part of their souls.

Then he found that the divine ecstasy he had awakened in Samala was what he felt and was so unique and so rapturous that he was sure he too was in a dream.

"I . . . love you . . . I love . . . you!" Samala murmured against his lips.

As he responded he knew that the words had a deeper meaning than they had ever had for him before in all the years he had been a man.

"I love and worship you, my perfect little wife!" he murmured.

Then the sunshine enveloped them with a dazzling light and the angels were singing.

* * *

A long time later, when the heat of the sun had gone and the rooks were going to roost amongst the trees in the Park, Samala said:

"I am . . . so happy . . . that I am . . . afraid!"

The Duke pulled her a little closer to him and said:

"You must never be afraid again. I will look after you, protect you, and keep you safe as long as we both shall live."

"I am only afraid that . . . everything is too perfect, because God has . . . answered all my . . . prayers."

He pulled her closer still, and as she lifted her face to his, she said:

"I prayed that He would make you . . . love me a little . . . just a very little . . . because I love . . . you so much, but now I can hardly . . . believe that you . . . love me as you say . . . you do."

"It is something I am very willing to prove," the Duke replied, "and, my darling, we have a long time in which I can do so, and we have a great many things to do together."

"I know that is what I have . . . wanted you to say," Samala said, "but I have been so . . . afraid that you would find me a . . . bore or inadequate, and would want to fill your life with . . . other exciting people rather than just me."

Vaguely the Duke seemed to remember that that was what he had intended, but now everything he had thought of and planned before he met Samala seemed to have drifted away into a mist.

All he could think of was that she was his, and he could not believe that anything in the whole world could be so exciting as holding her in his arms and teaching her about love.

"I am going to take you away from here," he said, "as soon as we feel well enough to travel, to one of my other houses, which is very quiet, and no-one will interrupt us."

Samala gave a cry of joy. Then she said in a low voice:

"You have forgotten . . . something."

"What is it?"

"It is Ascot . . . next week."

The Duke laughed.

"I really had forgotten, but it is not important. I will send my horses, and I hope they win several races, including the Gold Cup, but you and I will not be there."

Samala stared up at him incredulously.

"Do you really . . . mean . . . that?"

"I am going on my honeymoon," the Duke said firmly, "and I have a special prize of my own to collect."

Samala hid her face against him.

"Now," she said in a broken little voice, "I know . . . you really . . . love me."

"I will make love to you, my little angel," the Duke answered, "until you never doubt that again."

Then he added softly, as if he spoke to himself:

"But I must not frighten you."

"How could you do . . . that?" Samala asked. "When you loved me just now it was . . . so glorious . . . so thrilling . . . I wanted you to go on forever and ever!"

The Duke laughed, but very tenderly.

"What did you feel?"

"As if . . . all the stars were . . . twinkling inside me!"

"And it made you happy?"

"I did not know that . . . love was so perfect and that . . . God could lift us up into Heaven and make us . . . one with . . . Him."

"Is that really what I made you feel?"

"That, and so much more," she said. "When you loved me there was the music of the angels and the scent of the flowers which I had always known were in Heaven, but then there was only you . . . and your love."

She paused, then asked tentatively:

"Did you . . . feel anything . . . like that?"

The Duke kissed her forehead before he answered:

"You promised me a present from the Heavenly spheres, and that, my darling, adorable little wife, is what you gave me."

Samala gave one of her little cries of joy before she said:

"Do you mean . . . that? Do you really . . . mean that I gave you . . . something which . . . nobody else has ever . . . given you . . . before?"

"I swear to you that is the truth," the Duke said, "and, darling, nothing I can give you could be so precious or so perfect."

As he spoke, his lips found hers again, and as he felt her love vibrate towards him and become part of his vibrations, he knew that the life they would live together in the future would be very different from anything he had done in the past.

Just as he vowed to himself that he would protect her, so he knew that to do so he must live up to all the ideals with which she had endowed him from the moment she had seen him ride in the Steeple-Chase.

He was her Knight, her Crusader, and she must never be disillusioned.

He put his arms round her, and looking down at her said very gently:

"I know now, my precious, that our marriage was made in Heaven. That is where we will keep it, and as our love is a part of God we will never lose it."

Even as he spoke he thought that those were very strange words for him to utter, but they came from his soul, which had never been owned by any woman before, but which he knew now was Samala's.

"I love you . . . I love you!" Samala cried.

As the Duke's heart beat against hers, and his lips kissed her, and his hands touched her body, she felt once again as if he were carrying her into Heaven.

The music of the angels vibrated in the air, and they were enveloped with the Divine Light which is the power and perfection of Love.

ABOUT THE AUTHOR

BARBARA CARTLAND is the bestselling authoress in the world, according to the *Guinness Book of World Records*. She has sold over 200 million books and has beaten the world record for five years running, last year with 24 and the previous years with 24, 20, and 23.

She is also an historian, playwright, lecturer, political speaker and television personality, and has now written over 320 books.

She has also had many historical works published and has written four autobiographies as well as the biographies of her mother and that of her brother, Ronald Cartland, who was the first Member of Parliament to be killed in the last war. This book has a preface by Sir Winston Churchill and has just been republished with an introduction by Sir Arthur Bryant.

Love at the Helm, a novel written with the help and inspiration of the late Earl Mountbatten of Burma, Uncle of His Royal Highness Prince Philip, is being sold for the Mountbatten Memorial Trust.

In 1978 Miss Cartland sang an Album of Love Songs with the Royal Philharmonic Orchestra.

She is unique in that she was #1 and #2 in the Dalton List of Bestsellers, and one week had four books in the top twenty.

In private life Barbara Cartland, who is a Dame of the Order of St. John of Jerusalem, Chairman of the St. John Council in Hertfordshire and Deputy President of the St. John Ambulance Brigade, has also fought for better conditions and salaries for midwives and nurses.

As President of the Royal College of Midwives (Hertfordshire Branch) she has been invested with the first badge of Office ever given in Great Britain, whoch was subscribed to by the midwives themselves.

Barbara Cartland is deeply interested in vitamin therapy and is President of the British National Association for Health. Her book, *The Magic of Honey*, has sold throughout the world and is translated into many languages.

Seventy four newspapers in the United States and several countries in Europe carry strip cartoons of Barbara Cartland's novels.